I0671879

TEMPTING TESSA

BLACK SWAN DIVISION SERIES, BOOK 2

MISTY EVANS
NOLAN EVANS

Beach
Path
Publishing

ACKNOWLEDGMENTS

Many thanks to all those readers who've supported this new series. It's so good to be back in the spy world!

A special thank you to Amanda, Billie Jo, and JoAn in my private reader group for your YouTube watching and liking of my recent videos and the interview I did with Michelle Miles! You're the best!

BLACK SWAN DEFINITION

A black swan is an unpredictable event beyond what is typically expected of a situation and has potentially severe consequences.

Black swan events are characterized by their extreme rarity, severe impact, and the widespread insistence they were obvious in hindsight.

Unmask the Shadows. Face the Truth. Survive the Impossible.

The *Black Swan Division* thriller series is a pulse-pounding blend of high-stakes espionage, gritty action, and unforgettable characters.

When the world's most volatile threats demand a response beyond the reach of conventional forces, the Black Swan Division answers the call.

Led by fearless undercover operative Meg Carson

and her enigmatic second-in-command Declan Reid, this elite CIA team specializes in missions no one else can handle—missions where failure isn't an option.

From international conspiracies to rogue assassins, the team navigates deadly terrains, all while wrestling with fractured loyalties, personal demons, and secrets that could destroy them from within.

The *Black Swan Division* series delivers heart-stopping twists, nonstop action, and a dash of slow-burn romance. Each book draws you deeper into a web of deception, daring escapes, and the kind of heroism that tests the limits of trust and courage.

Join the mission. The Black Swan Division is waiting.

ONE

Bucharest, Romania

THE WRONG GUY was in her bed.

Again.

Tommy Mendoza slept peacefully on his stomach, his brown curls in a messy array around his head, one arm thrown out toward her pillow, the other hanging off the edge of the mattress.

Tessa leaned against the door jamb, sipping her morning coffee, and enjoyed the view. Moments like this, where she could watch him without him realizing it, were rare. Since he'd unexpectedly shown up at her door, he'd created more than a few problems for her. Several criminal organizations were after him. Assassins were hunting him. Along with that, the CIA's Black Swan Division, a highly classified group of trained "fixers," wanted him brought in for questioning.

Why do I keep doing this to myself?

The devil on her shoulder, who sounded like her high school best friend, Sarah, replied, "Because you like tempting fate."

Fair enough. She tempted fate daily, but she'd left the CIA and wasn't keen on returning. The only reason she'd helped the swans on their last mission to recover a USB from the Romanian embassy was out of honor for her dead friend—and Tommy's sister—Jessie.

Being in the precarious position of having a crush on the younger man while feeling like a traitor to Meg, Declan, and Spence by not telling them that Tommy was in her apartment, she had to reconsider where her loyalties lay.

Taking one more long look at Tommy's muscled back and tousled hair that she itched to run her fingers through, she pushed off the jam and silently closed the door.

She refilled her cup in the kitchen and sat at the center island, where her Sig Sauer waited for her. Earbuds in, she dialed Meg Carson's number and began dismantling the gun to clean it.

The other end rang three times before the leader of the black swans answered. "You do realize it's midnight here, right?" Meg asked with a yawn.

"In bed already?"

She heard the sounds of Meg rising from the mattress and moving into another room, leaving Declan Reid, her lover and second in command, behind. "I ran seven miles today and then did an hour of shooting practice. On top of that, I got to spend three hours this afternoon in meetings with Flynn, Stone, and a bunch of analysts. The best part? Flynn made me keep my mouth shut."

Tessa chuckled. Of all those tasks, the last one had to have been the hardest for the team leader. Meg was never one to hold back her thoughts. She was opinionated, highly intelligent, and could probably outthink most of the attendees at the meeting. "And you wonder why I don't want to return to the fold."

"Any leads on Tommy?"

Straight to it, then. The first part of the swans' assignment had been recovering the USB. The second was to find Jessie's brother, who had uncovered an impending EMP attack at multiple military facilities worldwide.

Tessa glanced toward the bedroom as she used her cloth to wipe down the face of the chamber. "He's keeping a low profile. Tell me again what happened when Mosai Hagar captured you and Jessie."

"Why?"

Because something didn't make sense to her about all of it. "Humor me. You were in Vienna, rounding up expats on Scepter's hit list."

The sounds of Meg getting a glass of water filtered through the phone. "There were a few who refused to leave, like Captain Ulee. He was too high profile for the US to risk him being taken alive and tortured by Scepter for information, so we were instructed to *encourage* his evacuation, along with a few others. Declan and Spence handled him, and Jessie and I stayed behind to keep eyes on Urich Scepter and his group."

That was when Hagar and his death squad had snatched her and Jessie. "How did Hagar know who you were and your whereabouts? Why did he want you and Jessie?"

"The only people who were supposed to know about our mission were Flynn, Stone, Del, and a few state department plants in Vienna. All CIA. All were questioned and above suspicion. As stated in Flynn's report to the Director and Deputy Director, we believe someone picked up one of our secure communications, figured out what was going on, and forwarded that information to Hagar. He'd had a vendetta against the US since the Iraq invasion. Eliminating CIA operatives was his favorite sport."

And still... "You and Jessie were no ordinary operatives. The swans are ghosts. Only a handful of people in the entire world know about you."

"Supposedly," Meg said with derision. "Hagar probably informed every one of his buddies and potentially the Russian investors who are backing the EMP attacks about our true identities."

Tessa checked the clip and laid it on the towel, eyeing the separate pieces that would once more form a weapon when she put them back together. Every part had a purpose, and without even one of them, the gun would not fire properly, if at all.

Her nickname within CIA circles was The Architect. She had never taken to undercover work like she had to inserting deception into buildings. Hidden rooms, secret tunnels, invisible back doors—these were her craft.

Every building needed a strong and balanced foundation to support its framework. Every piece of wood, section of concrete, and piece of pipe played a role in creating a whole, solid structure.

This was how she looked at everything, from the weapon lying in front of her and the buildings she helped the CIA design with hidden entries and exits to missions and operations. The design needed to be flawless in order to avoid weaknesses, and each component had to work well with the others.

Meg, Dec, and Spence were like her Sig—they formed a cohesive and deadly weapon. Jessie had been part of that, and with her gone, they were looking at Tessa to replace her.

Hiding Tommy from them was a dangerous game, but she owed him more than she cared to. Jessie had been one of her closest friends. Tessa had taken her under her wing when Jessie and Meg showed up at The Farm seven years ago, seeing the potential each brought to the table.

Tessa and Meg had both been close to Jessie, but Meg's guilt over Jessie's death was as much about responsibility as it was about friendship. Tessa didn't carry that guilt, but she wanted revenge for Jessie's death equally as much.

Which was why she was tempting fate by helping Tommy while lying to Meg. "Why did Hagar pick Jessie to execute first? He knew you were the team leader—why wouldn't he put you on camera for his public execution?"

Meg sighed, and Tessa imagined her leaning against her kitchen counter. "I've asked myself that a thousand times. I don't know. He kept us in these tiny cages, like dog kennels. He tortured us and sent a video of the torture sessions to the CIA. He treated me as horrifically as he did her. Maybe something she said to him that day pushed him over the edge. She was constantly taunting him, angering him."

The bastard had made swift work of the execution, using his machete on Jessie with the cameras rolling live to several social media sites before it could be shut down.

Although the CIA had managed to remove any recorded section within minutes of the live broadcast, plenty of copies were still out there. Tessa had watched one multiple times, barely able to distinguish that it was even Jessie that Hagar killed with one mighty swing. She and Meg had only been with him and his death squad a week, but the damage he'd done to them physically had left them nearly unrecognizable.

She hated to imagine what Meg still wrestled with mentally and emotionally, even now that the bastard was dead.

"He was too calculating for that," Tessa mused, more to herself than to Meg. "And you were already under his control. More torture would have been a normal response to her provocations."

"Killing operatives was personal. Revenge for the US taking out his family during one of the raids in Iraq. I don't think strategy won against his rage that day."

He'd been the lone survivor. "Why would Jessie taunt him?"

"Because she wouldn't be cowed. Ever."

True. "Did she not hope for rescue?"

Meg's pause was long and weighted. "No."

"But you did?"

"I worked on an escape plan. I failed."

Tessa understood the burden of that. She'd failed plenty in her lifetime, too. Never with a teammate's life, though.

Her fingers moved with ease as she finished putting the Sig to rights. "You're sure Jessie had no prior connection to Hagar?"

Another pause, this one more inquisitive. "What are you suggesting?"

Tessa sipped coffee. What she was about to say might cause Meg to hate her. "I'm suggesting that Jessie knew Hagar before the kidnapping. She potentially leaked your whereabouts to him for reasons we may never know, but she had information on him that he didn't want to get out. Something or someone alerted him that Declan and Spence were about to swoop in and rescue the two of you, so he killed her first because he needed to silence her."

And then he'd escaped.

Tessa heard the bedroom door open.

"You can't be serious," Meg hissed in her ears.

She was.

Glancing toward the bedroom, she found Tommy staring at her with his dark, damaged eyes.

All of it led back to him.

The man wanted by so many and who'd been sleeping in her bed.

TWO

Tired, sore, and battling a fissure of suspicion spreading in his gut, Tommy propped himself against the door frame, eyes locked on Tessa. She'd been cleaning her gun, the parts now reassembled. Seeing his gaze burning a hole in her, she picked up her cup of coffee, all casual-like, and sipped.

The hand holding the cup trembled slightly, though. That's what made the fissure of suspicion deepen. Her expression stayed smooth, giving nothing away, and her eyes slid over him with a warm appraisal. The corner of her mouth quirked as she met his gaze. She could disarm people like that—distracting them with nothing more than a careful assessment or interested yet neutral expression. Appearing so in control that most never noticed the cracks underneath.

Tommy had learned how to see the cracks. He'd honed his ability to sense danger. It was the only way he'd been able to survive so far.

"Who are you talking to?" His voice came out rough and groggy from sleep. He wondered if she noticed the suspicion layered under it.

She disconnected the call. "No one important," she replied, slipping out one earbud. She didn't explain further, which meant the answer *was* important, probably someone she didn't want him to know about.

Not tough to guess. Meg Carson.

He was running for his life, every step shadowed by the CIA and dangerous terrorists. All of them playing games.

But it was one of the reasons he'd come to her. She was used to dabbling in these kinds of games. Not dabbling, per se, but never genuinely invested in undercover work. He wondered if she ever invested all of her interest in anything. Yet, here he was, relying on her.

The one person he shouldn't trust.

What has she told Meg? That he was here? That she'd stitched his wound and was letting him sleep in her bed?

Nothing had happened between them, and a part of him was sorry about that. Under different circumstances, he would do just about anything to strip her naked and get her under him, but right now, he had too many killers breathing down his neck. There was no way he had time or energy for a relationship.

Besides, she would become one more weakness. One more person he needed to protect.

"You talk in your sleep," he said, pushing off the doorframe and sauntering into the kitchen. He ran a hand through his hair as he found a mug to fill with coffee.

"No, I don't."

He turned, inhaling the dark brew, and braced a hand on the counter as he leaned against it. "You didn't know? I suppose it's a bad attribute when you're a spy— spilling secrets to lovers without even knowing it."

She cocked her head, feline-like. Unconcerned but curious. "What secret did I reveal?"

"Nothing actionable." He dropped into the chair at the island next to her. The aftertaste of coffee sat on his tongue, as bitter as the thought she might have betrayed him. "You were muttering about Hager and Jessie." He gestured with his chin toward her phone. "I'm guessing this early morning call wasn't about a recipe swap."

Her gaze flipped to her Sig Sauer, then back to him. He could almost see the calculations going on behind those beautiful eyes. Should she deny calling Meg? Deflect his question? Come clean?

He'd been around plenty of spies, including his sister, but Tessa was the one that consistently fascinated him. She seemed to walk between worlds, never committing fully to any.

Setting aside her cup, she picked up the cloth and wiped nonexistent grime from the gun barrel. "Do you think Jessie knew something about the EMP attacks?"

Deflection it was. He'd overheard what she'd said to Meg. He also understood where that suspicion about his sister came from. He'd been wrestling with it himself.

Saying it out loud and discussing it, even with Tessa, somehow made it real. His gut tightened, but he pushed past the hard, unforgiving lump. There would be no relief until he confronted it directly.

He wasn't one to shy away from unpleasant and disturbing revelations. "It's the only thing that makes sense: that she was investigating the possibility, searching for proof, and following leads."

Or worse, something far more sinister.

That was one revelation he wasn't ready to divulge yet, though. He'd never known Jessie to be anything other than upstanding and loyal to the Black Swans and The Agency. To even suspect her of wrongdoing went against every fiber of his being. *She would never do such a thing.*

He hoped. Prayed. Insisted to that nagging voice inside his head. *Never.*

Staring at her gun but seeming lost in her thoughts, Tessa nodded once. "Why didn't you tell us?"

What she really meant was, *Why didn't you tell me?*

He hesitated, then pushed past the heaviness of betrayal again. "It's not every day you discover your sister might have had knowledge of such a devasting event being planned and realize she didn't trust you enough to share it."

Her gaze shot to his, locking on him like a laser. "Jessie trusted you. Out of all of us, you were her best friend. Her confidant."

The question she had been wrestling with echoed her earlier one. "So why didn't she tell me?"

Tessa reached for his hand, resting beside his cup, and squeezed it. "She was brutally logical. Maybe she didn't have enough evidence to proceed, so there was no reason to burden you with it."

He felt her surety, her confidence in Jessie through the squeeze. She wanted it to be true, just like he did. Maybe between the two of them, they could will it into being. "She did have proof."

"How can you be sure?"

He swung around on the barstool to face her, his knees bumping her leg. They were so close, their current living situation so intimate, yet he couldn't take advantage of it. He wanted to kiss her, to taste the coffee on her tongue, to drag her back to the bedroom and do what he had wanted to do these past few nights—peel the straps of her nightgown off her shoulders, kiss her collarbone, cup her breasts. He wanted to kiss her until her lips were swollen. Do things to her that made her cry out his name.

But he couldn't. Not only had she been Jessie's friend, but she had no interest in him. Not like that. The warm appraisals of his body were to keep him off guard. To determine if she could trust him. She might have appreciated his male physique, but he knew underneath that it was just another game to her.

Where did her true loyalties lie? With her friend's brother or with the swans and the CIA? Should he be suspicious of that phone call? Was someone going to show up here any minute to arrest him and take him back to the States?

"The USB," he told her. "She did come to me, just not directly. I found it in my desk a few days after her funeral. She must've hidden it there before Vienna."

"And you figured out what was on it. The information about Hagar."

"I was digging into an investment firm in Russia and following a money trail I believed backed up my suspicions about his involvement in the impending EMP attacks. Attacks that Jessie knew about. She knew about the superconductors for the military's computers being tampered with."

EMP bombs—e-bombs—had been around for years, the US being one of the countries at the forefront of designing non-nuclear tools to destroy information systems. They'd created devices small enough to fit in a briefcase, making them feasible and practical.

The Defense Department's reliance on satellites and commercial computer equipment to command military forces and operations worldwide was threatened. Much had been done to take precautions to offset such attacks.

Still, if what Tommy, via Jessie's intel, had uncovered, the superconductors used in military computers having been tampered with would leave the bases fucked. America's infrastructure, as well. It would bring on a type of apocalypse that could cause the collapse of many countries' systems worldwide.

"Like you said, Jessie was logical," Tommy continued. "She had proof, but she wanted all the players exposed so that when she handed this information to Flynn and the others, they had everything they needed to round up the entire ring. She knew that leaving even one of them free could still jeopardize our military and our country. He swung back to face the counter, toying with his coffee cup. "She traveled off the grid for two weeks, meeting with someone before Vienna. I've been chasing her steps ever since."

"Where did she go?"

"Ilford, outside of London, then she went to Arizona."

"I know where Ilford is. What's there?"

"An energy company."

"And Arizona?"

He rubbed his thumb up and down the side of the cup. "There are two computer companies outside of Tucson. Both commercial organizations."

She must have heard the doubt in his tone. "But...?"

"MediSune is a cover for Cal Line, a secret branch dedicated to researching and developing supercomputers for the military. MediSune makes and sells computer systems to the public, but they focus on city and county governments. Their private branch is undocumented, and I have no idea how she uncovered the information, but probably through an informant inside the CIA or Department of Defense. They are the only ones who know about the site and would have that information."

"That's where it all started, the sabotage of the superconductors."

He nodded. "That USB is heavily encrypted, and there were parts of it that I couldn't even get to, but there was more involving a Russian shell company funding paramilitary groups and a man named Viktor. No last name. I believe it was an alias. The same alias popped up on some financial transactions linked to that Russian shell company."

"Jessie was tracking the network behind the EMP plot, and she knew Hager was their lead guy. She probably figured he might know Viktor's true identity."

Tommy gestured at her phone. "That's why she taunted him. You're right to suspect it wasn't simply defiance. Jessie wanted Hagar to slip up and confirm something—possibly Viktor's identity or something else. I don't know, but I need to retrace her footsteps. Follow her path to Ilford and Arizona."

He left it sitting there—an invitation.

But it was more than that. He needed Tessa's help.

She sat back, crossing her arms. "You've been on the run for weeks, and you're still recovering from being shot." Her gaze flicked to his bandaged side and back to his face. "Assassins, Russians, the CIA...they're all after you, and now, you want to waltz into London and then fly to America to chase this Viktor fellow? Do you have a death wish?"

"You think I don't know what the risks are?"

"I think you're being foolish. The CIA has the thumb drive, and they're decoding it. They'll have all the info Jessie put on it in a matter of days, maybe a week or two, tops. Your quest is not only dangerous, it's stupid. Go to Langley, talk to Flynn, and let the professionals handle it."

He slammed a hand on the counter, causing the cups to jump. "Hagar's dead, Tessa. I didn't even get to pull the trigger. And the network that put all of this in motion has probably accelerated their timeline because of it. We may not have weeks, and the Agency moves like a crippled dinosaur. If I turn myself in, I'll end up spending months being interrogated, and nothing will be accomplished."

"Flynn fully understands the emergency this creates. He's already got the heads of Homeland, the Justice Department, and the Feds working to ensure those computers are confiscated and the bases secured."

"It's not enough," he growled. "Even if they deter the e-bombs, they won't bring down the network. Those involved have probably already gone to ground. They'll begin eliminating anyone who can identify them. I have to flush them out. Now. Or everything Jessie did—her death—will have been in vain."

Her expression didn't soften, but guilt and sympathy flashed in her eyes. "You're good, Tommy, but you're not a trained undercover operative. You need help."

It was a gift—his ability to sense when someone was crumbling. "Help me, Tessa. You owe her that much."

She glared at him, then looked away, jaw set. "Don't you dare."

"We both made promises to our country and to her. Ones we didn't keep."

"You don't get to use her to manipulate me."

Frustration boiled over, and he stood, nearly toppling the stool. "I'm reminding you of what's at stake. Jessie gave her life to bring down this organization. The work is left undone. It's up to me—and you—to see it through. If she were here, she'd ask you to do it."

"She's *not* here." Her voice cut like a blade. She dropped her head into her hands, her voice lowering. "If you keep charging into every fight like this, you won't be either."

The kitchen was silent for a moment, except for their breathing.

He'd thought she was crumbling. That she would give in. Stupid of him. He headed for the bedroom to pack. "I'll be out of your hair in a minute."

His frustration continued to boil until his head felt like it would explode. Jamming the few clothes he had into his backpack, he checked his weapon and stuck it into the waistband of his pants. He was out of money, had nowhere to go in Ilford, and his side hurt like a son of a bitch.

But his own words rang in his ears. If Jessie were here, she would keep going until she uncovered every last bastard who was part of the plot. She wouldn't wait for the Agency, the Department of Defense, Homeland, the FBI, or anyone else to do what needed to be done. She would do it.

"What exactly do you need from me?"

He whirled to see Tessa standing on the threshold. Her shoulders were tight, her mouth, too.

Relief flooded him, but he kept his tone even. "I need you to help me retrace Jessie's steps. I don't have the contacts to navigate London and Ilford. You do."

She kept her feet braced and crossed her arms. The movement boosted her breasts. "If I do this, it doesn't mean I'm returning to the CIA or avoiding them. I will not betray them or my country. I'm not letting you drag me into your personal vendetta, but I realize the enormity of the situation. If I can do something to prevent it from happening, then I wouldn't be able to live with myself if I didn't do it."

"If you have to tell Meg the truth, I understand. But doing so could compromise my mission."

"You leave Meg to me. There's always a way to work with the swans without compromising anything, and I'll take care of that. Ilford and the technology company are probably a dead end. You know that, right?"

"Do you have a better idea?"

She marched across the room to her closet and grabbed a go-bag. "In fact, I do. We do this my way. No improvising and no lone-wolf stunts. Understand?"

Was it possible he wasn't alone in this fight for the first time since Jessie's death? "For now."

She smirked at him, rolling her eyes, and he trailed after her as she returned to the kitchen, retrieving her gun. "Don't make me shoot you, Tommy."

He grinned. Not teasing her was too hard. "No promises on that."

THREE

Tessa pulled the hood of her jacket tighter against the misty drizzle as she led Tommy down the shadowed alley. The uneven cobblestones, slick with rain, demanded her attention, and she'd already twisted her ankle once but didn't slow her pace.

Behind her, his footsteps thudded louder than necessary. He was angry, and his frustration reverberated off the walls. "Skipping Ilford is a mistake," he muttered. "That's where Jessie started. We shouldn't bypass it."

Men. They were always so...annoying. "We're not skipping it," she replied over her shoulder. "We're re-prioritizing. The computer lab in Arizona is the key. It's the bigger breadcrumb, so that's our end goal, just like it seems to have been for her. If we have time and means, we can check into Ilford on our way through London."

Tommy brushed past her to block her path. She stopped just short of colliding with him. He had his hood up, too, but the mist had collected on his unruly beard.

Above it, his sharp cheekbones emphasized his blue eyes as they bore into hers. "How exactly do you plan on getting me into the States? The CIA has my passport flagged. The second I use it, I'll light up Del's warning system like a damn Christmas tree."

Surely, he had put two and two together already. "That's why we're getting you a new one." She stepped around him and continued marching down the alley.

"Gee, why didn't I think of that?" He jogged to catch up. "Because fake documents have never gone sideways for anyone before when the CIA is looking for them."

She ignored his sarcasm, stopping shy of the street that would take them to the place they needed. She jammed a finger into his chest. "You came to me, remember? You're alive because of me. I told you we were going to do this my way, and you agreed. While I have a dog in this fight because I was friends with Jessie, and because I..." She couldn't finish. She *what*? Had feelings for him? Felt responsible for him?

Why the hell was she doing this? Why was she getting sucked back into undercover work and acting like an operative? Just like she had insisted to Flynn and Meg, she didn't do this stuff anymore. Sure, helping the swans with the Romanian Embassy problem had been exciting, but now she was knee-deep in shit she didn't want to be shoveling.

"Are you going to finish that sentence?" the man pulling her into the shit asked.

Annoying... "If I say we're going to Arizona, we're

going to Arizona. Now shut up, get out of my way, and let's get on with it."

For a tense moment, he stared down at her, his lips pressed into a hard line. Angry, cunning, deadly determined. This was the Tommy who'd been on the run, dodging assassins and terrorists. Hunting for his sister's killer only to discover he'd been denied his revenge.

While she wasn't sure, she suspected he hated Meg and Declan. Maybe even Spence. They'd let Hagar kill Jessie.

At least, that's what he believed.

She hadn't been there and didn't know anything other than what Spence had told her. Meg and Jessie had been ambushed, kidnapped, and beaten nearly to death. Declan could have saved Jessie but had chosen to save Meg that day instead.

Dec had been in a no-win situation. How did you choose between two teammates when their lives were on the line?

She returned Tommy's glare, refusing to back down. While she wasn't above laying blame at Dec's feet, she knew him to be one of the most dependable and reliable men she'd ever known. She knew the grief that they all carried and, for some stupid reason, felt her own healthy amount of it. She wasn't a swan, and yet...

Had she missed something along the way? Had Jessie said or done anything that she should have picked up on? When she'd learned that Hagar and his death squad had kidnapped Meg and Jessie, should she have left Romania and her simple life as a librarian behind and jumped back into the foray?

The answer was yes. Always yes.

It was too late to change what had happened. She would have to live with the questions and the guilt they brought.

Tommy exhaled through his nose, wiped a hand over his face, and just like that, his demeanor changed. He was back to being her Tommy—a man dealing with the fallout of his sister's death and still holding it together. A man who wanted to save the world.

A man she wanted to make smile.

He grumbled something under his breath about her being worse than Jessie. She took that as a compliment.

Not even attempting to keep the smile off her face, she resumed walking, his string of colorful curses following her. A block down the street, she stopped in front of a nondescript shop, its windows filled with a garish mix of blinking neon lights. A hand-painted sign above the door proclaimed in English, *Authentic Romanian Souvenirs.*

Tommy glanced up and down the nearly empty street. The place was so far off the beaten tourist path that few customers frequented the place. His voice came out low and incredulous. "This is where we're getting the passport?"

"Beggars can't be choosers."

"It looks like a postcard puked."

That it did. "It has a certain charm."

He snorted. She pushed the door open to the chime

of an outdated bell. Inside, the shop smelled of stale air and cheap incense. Shelves were cluttered with ceramic Dracula figurines, embroidered tablecloths, and touristy trinkets. A radio crackled faintly behind the counter, broadcasting a local talk show.

A man in his fifties appeared from the back room, the beaded curtain clacking as he shoved it aside, and it fell back to cover the opening. His belly strained against the buttons of his plaid shirt, and his balding head was artfully covered with a few long strands of what he had left of hair.

When he saw Tessa, his fake smile for tourists faded, and his lips covered his nicotine-stained teeth. He cursed, albeit in Romanian. It seemed she was getting a lot of that today. His gaze went to Tommy, sizing him up. He switched to English when he spoke to Tessa. "What do you want?"

"Is that any way to greet one of your best customers, Vasile? Especially one who has helped you out of a jam more than once. Or have you forgotten those special memories?"

He rolled his eyes, forcing another fake smile as he dropped his Romanian accent. "Greetings. What can I do for you today, my favorite customer?"

"That's better." She moved to a display of traditional Romanian clothing and picked up a delicate veil embroidered with crimson flowers. She draped it over her arm, her movements deliberate. His smile faltered, but his eyes lit up. The veil was worth less than twenty dollars, but what it signified was worth far more.

"Beautiful hand-stitching on that one," he said, now the consummate salesman. "The color will look good on you."

Tommy peered between them, not understanding the code but realizing there was one. Tessa stroked the veil. Only one other customer was in the shop, busy eyeing some coins. The man told Vasile he'd be back for the boxed collection and made for the exit, but she stayed in character. "Perhaps you have a mirror in the back that I could use to decide whether it's right or not for me?"

The bell tinkled as the coin connoisseur exited. Vasile gestured for them to step around the counter and follow him. "This way."

Tommy hesitated as the curtain swung aside again. She gave him a pointed look, and his forehead creased with the battle inside his mind. Should he follow? Should he trust her? Should he head to London on his own?

Decision made, he smoothed out his frown and followed Vasile.

The back room was cramped, lit by a single bulb hanging from the ceiling. There were boxes of inventory, a decrepit desk with papers and an ancient typewriter against one wall, and a small cabinet with a large TV on top of it. The picture showed a soccer game, but the sound was turned off.

They wove around stacked boxes as he brought them into an even smaller room. He closed the door behind them and held up his arms to avoid touching them as he squeezed past and made his way to the desk.

Everything was high-tech here. A computer,

multiple printers, a light table, a camera on an adjustable tripod, and a screen on the wall vied for space. "Who needs the papers," he asked, "and what kind?"

Tessa hitched a thumb toward Tommy. "Him. Heath Mathers. American. Passport and American driver's license from Arizona." She pulled a piece of paper from her pocket. "Here are the details. He also needs pages that show he's been traveling internationally for the past year."

"Locations?" the man asked.

"Mostly Europe. Nothing South of the border."

He slipped a pair of reading glasses on his nose, eyeing Tommy with mild disdain. "He looks like a homeless lumberjack. Even with papers, no one will believe he's anything but trouble."

Tessa smirked. "He *is* trouble, but that's not your concern."

Tommy issued a tight huff. "Will the two of you stop talking about me as if I'm not here?"

"You haven't said anything useful," Vasile replied. "Do you always let her do all the talking?"

Tommy looked like he might punch the guy in the face. "I can't shut her up. Budapest, Vienna, here. Those are the places to put in my passport."

The man dismissed him with a glance at her. "This will take time and money."

"Half now, half when it's done," Tessa said. She pulled a bundle of euros from her backpack. This was their standard agreement, but she always insisted on being clear with instructions. "We're in a hurry. I need the papers today."

Vasile grumbled in both Romanian and English. "I'm good, but I need more time."

He always said that. "I'm about to take him next door and make your wife very happy. You do want her to be happy, don't you, Vasile? You start the documentation, and we'll return for the picture shortly."

"What's next door?" Tommy asked.

She laid the veil on the desk next to the money. It would be a nice souvenir for Meg. "I'll take this too." Grabbing Tommy's arm, she pulled him to the exit. "Time for your makeover."

FOUR

The salon smelled of hairspray and citrus shampoo. The walls were painted a nauseating shade of pink, and a chandelier made of plastic crystals dangled precariously overhead.

Tommy sat in the chair, scowling at his reflection as the stylist—a stout woman with expertly dyed blond and purple-streaked hair—clipped away at his overgrown locks.

"Not so short," he snapped, wincing as she ran the clippers close to his ear.

"You are lucky I don't have to use my garden shears," she snapped back in a thick accent.

"Stop being a baby," Tessa said. Inches of his hair fell to the floor. She paced behind him, her mouth quirked to one side in thought. He saw her chewing the inside of her cheek as she strategized their next move.

It was sexy as hell.

She might claim that she hated the spy world and

wanted nothing more to do with any of it, but she was damn good at this stuff. She had connections Meg didn't. She knew how people thought and how to manipulate them without violence or threats. At least, nothing *directly* threatening. She liked it when people owed her favors. When they felt indebted.

He wondered how much he would be indebted to her when this was over.

If I get out alive, I'll give her anything she wants.

Was it too much to hope that she wanted him?

Not as a friend. At least not only as one.

Fantasy, that. She was older, wiser, and saw him as nothing but a kid. Jessie's little brother. He'd never shake that label.

Not that he wanted to. Jessie had been his hero growing up. They'd survived so much together—losing their parents and being shuffled around from one foster home to another. Jessie had made sure they were together more than they were apart, but there'd been times when even she couldn't override the system. She'd gotten good at running away, though. Running away and finding him.

Throughout it all, she'd brought him books, games, and food. She'd insisted he read philosophy, poetry, and history. Most of it he hated, but he would've done anything to make his sister proud.

Now, he wished he could thank her. Tell her how much he appreciated what she'd done for them, for him. Just to see her one more time, put his arms around her.

Sorina finished with his hair but refused to spin him around so he could see himself in her mirror. "*Da?*" she said to Tessa, gesturing at him with her dagger-like nails. "Better?"

Tessa eyeballed him. "He looks... Older. Smarter. I'll get him some glasses."

He tried to pivot in the seat, but Sorina blocked him, picking up a different pair of scissors. "Now that disgusting beard."

He threw up a hand to block her. "I need to keep some facial hair. It's part of my disguise."

"Your disguise is blown after the embassy riots," Tessa told him. To the stylist, she said, "Trim it down to a ghost layer. Keep it neat."

"As you wish," the woman replied.

He flinched as she went to work again, her sharp scissors barely missing the end of his nose.

"Why don't I get a say in this?" he asked.

"You're the one who let your beard grow out like a mountain man," Tessa said, leaning against the checkout counter with her arms crossed, unamused.

"Still lucky I don't need my garden shears," Sorina said, not hiding her amusement as she whacked away at his cheeks and chin.

The minutes dragged as he forced himself to sit still. Sorina traded the scissors for clippers, the buzz filling his ears while Tessa regarded him without sympathy.

When the stylist finally stepped back, she rotated the chair, and Tommy blinked at himself. It was a shocking change to see the sides of his head trimmed close with only a few longer locks left on top. His beard was nothing more than a shadow on his jaw.

"Holy shit," he muttered. He hadn't looked this clean and upstanding since he'd posed for his State Department photo.

"You look like a respectable human being again," Tessa said, tilting her head as she examined him.

"Are you sure this is a good idea? I look like me again. If they catch me on camera, facial rec will ID me."

Tessa went behind a screen, and he heard her rummaging through drawers. She returned with a pair of round, wire-rimmed glasses and a small tote. When she opened the tote, he saw it contained a myriad of makeup and silicon facial features—eyebrows, cheek ridges, and chins. In the right hands, his face could be transformed.

Apparently, Tessa had the skills to do it. "Just some subtle tweaks," she said, winking at him. "If we change your brow bone, lower your earlobes, and thicken your cheekbones, that should be enough to fool most facial rec systems. You'll wear a cap and these glasses, too."

By the time she finished, he looked like himself—except not. She'd used makeup to blend in the artificial enhancements and added wrinkles, making him look at least ten years older.

She put away the case, tipped Sorina handsomely, and signaled him to stop gawking at himself in the mirror. "Time for your photo shoot."

Returning to the souvenir shop, Tommy stood where he was told to let the man snap his picture. Vasile angled the camera so that Tessa could peer at the photo.

She examined it with a critical eye. "You clean up

well," she said. Vasile had her veil wrapped and ready to go. She scooped it up. "We'll be back in two hours."

"Yeah, yeah." He waved her off. "Get out of here so I can work."

The rain had stopped, leaving the air damp and heavy. Tessa checked her watch. "Lunch?"

"Is it safe to be seen with me?"

Her critical gaze ran over him again. She touched one of his brows as if brushing off a stray hair. "I think you'll pass, Professor."

"Professor?"

"Yes. A distinguished college professor—that's what you remind me of."

The way she said it, as if the idea verged on a racy fantasy, made him stand a bit taller. "Of what? Philosophy? History? Science?" he asked, playing along.

"Literature, I think."

"Boring," he said.

"Sexy," she countered.

She didn't take him to any of the popular tourist hotspots. Instead, she led them into a tiny café on a side street, its windows slightly fogged from the warmth inside. They ordered bowls of soup and a plate of grilled meats, which arrived steaming and fragrant.

Wiping the moisture off the window with a napkin, Tommy scanned the street outside. He kept running a hand through his short hair and wondering how to make casual conversation. It had been too long since he'd had to act normal.

Tessa simply regarded him while she ate, seeming content with the silence.

The place was nearly empty. The gal behind the counter kept giving him flirty glances and even winked. He ignored her, watching the street for any sign of danger.

"You're paranoid," Tessa said, dipping a chunk of bread into her soup.

"Paranoia has kept me alive."

She nodded. "Relax. That's my job for now."

But halfway through their meal, his vigilance paid off. Across the street, he saw movement that made the remaining hair on his neck stand up. "Down!" He yelled just as a crack rang out and the window spiderwebbed.

Tessa hit the floor, and for half a second, his heart stopped dead in his chest. He thought she'd been shot, but as he joined her, pulling her to him, her eyes were wide, and she blinked at him.

Another shot punched through the remaining glass, embedding itself in the wall.

With barely a thought, he jerked her onto her hands and knees and shoved her forward. "Go," yelled. "Back door!"

She grabbed her backpack. The other patrons were screaming, and the girl behind the counter had disappeared. He couldn't take time to check and see if any of them were hit, scrambling to get Tessa to safety.

She shoved the back door open, and he saw a small gated area with a dumpster and two cars packed into a tiny patch of concrete. The vehicles had to belong to the waitress and the cook.

When he went to grab Tessa and head for the locked gate, she pointed. "Fire escape."

She was on it and climbing before he could argue.

As they scrambled to the roof, a bullet pinged off the metal steps below. Whoever was shooting wasn't far behind, but when he glanced down, all he saw was a hooded figure taking cover near the dumpster.

"What's your plan here," he said as they hit the roof, "*bodyguard.*"

"Shut up and run," she snapped, tugging him toward the edge.

He didn't like where this was going. "You can't be serious."

But she was. He watched with a mixture of shock and fascination as she launched herself off the building roof and onto the one next to it.

She fell into a controlled roll and bounced back up on her feet. Blood covered one of her arms. She *had* been shot.

"Coming?" she called. Was that a challenging grin on her face?

Gritting his teeth, he ran for the ledge and leaped.

FIVE

Tessa's breath hitched as they sprinted across the scaly, black-pitch rooftop. Her arm throbbed where the bullet had grazed her, the wet warmth of blood trickling down to her elbow. She clamped her free hand over the wound and swallowed a curse, forcing her legs to move, the backpack slapping against her side.

Behind her, Tommy kept pace, his footfalls quick on the tar-covered flat expanse.

She ducked behind one of the enormous HVAC units, taking a moment to catch her breath. His face was full of worry as he bent down beside her. "We can't stop here."

"Is she still following?"

A crease formed between his brows. "She? "

She nodded. "The shooter is female."

He looked like he wanted to question her about it, but there wasn't time. "You're hurt."

"Just a scratch." She shifted so she could peek around

the unit. The rain had picked up, and she wiped at her eyes. There was no one in sight, no sounds of pursuit. "I think it's clear."

He peered around the metal box with her. No one shot at them. That was good. "Could be a trick. They could be waiting for us to move before they do, too."

The muffled sounds of traffic filtered up from the street. She'd be happier if they could get to a more populated area. "Guess lunch was a bad idea."

He drew her back into their hiding spot and examined her arm. "You're sure it's only a graze?"

"That's the least of my worries at the moment, but yes, I'm fine."

He'd lost the glasses and looked less like a professor. "You need a doctor."

"No doctor. Come on." He tried to pull her back down when she stood, but she yanked free of his grip and hustled for the fire escape. Her analysis was correct—the shooter hadn't followed them onto the roof.

"They could be anywhere down there, waiting for us," he said, catching up to her.

The sky spit ran in her face. "Then we have to be fast and outthink them."

He shook his head as she hefted herself onto the metal steps. "Wait," he ordered. "I go first."

She started to argue but sensed it was pointless. What had just happened had scared him, and he needed to take control. She'd give him that for now. "Just don't get shot, okay?"

The narrow steps forced him to turn sideways as he

passed her. For a brief second, they were chest-to-chest, face-to-face. His intense gaze snagged hers, his makeover still something she had to get used to. She couldn't decide if she liked him better with his curls or without. She regretted that she hadn't been able to run her fingers through them before they'd been lobbed off.

The moment passed, and he descended the rickety metal staircase in leaps, leaving her behind. She hurried to catch up, annoyed that he was intentionally putting space between them in case the shooter was waiting in the alley or on the street. He was making himself a damn target, and she would take him to task for it later.

When she arrived at ground level, he was already in stealth mode, scanning the alley, checking around the corners to view the street, and lifting his gaze to the rooftop lines. "Clear," he said. "At least, as far as I can tell."

It was too soon to go pick up the passport, and she couldn't exactly stroll around with blood dripping off the end of her fingers. She picked at the frayed hole in her jacket and sighed. "This was my favorite," she complained under her breath.

Wiping blood off her hand and onto her jeans, she was thankful the pants were black so the red stains wouldn't show as much. Then she laced her clean fingers through Tommy's, startling him, and leaned against him like a lover. "I need to hide my wound while we make our way back to my place. Don't want to call attention to us."

He fished out a handkerchief and broke free from her

hand long enough to wad it up and shove it inside her sleeve. He was none too gentle, but she didn't mind, grateful that the fabric would soak up at least some of the oozing blood. Once he had it in place, his fingers brushed against her chest as he removed his hand. He zipped up her jacket and threaded his hand back through hers. Another of those intense moments passed between them as they stood together in the stinky alley. "Don't pass out on me from loss of blood, got it?" he groused.

She used her other hand to pat his cheek. "Who's giving the orders now?"

"This is not a joke, Tessa. Someone tried to kill you."

She pushed away from the wall and tugged him forward, raising her hood. It did no good against the rain but would help disguise her. "I'm not so sure about that."

They emerged on the busy street sidewalk, both of them keeping an eye out. "What do you mean?" he asked from the corner of his mouth. "You think they were shooting at me?"

She kept up the pretense of being his girlfriend, clinging to his arm as they skirted pedestrians with umbrellas going in the opposite direction. "I'm not sure who she was shooting at. Lousy shot if she was trying to actually kill either of us."

"She wounded you," he argued in that low tone.

"Only because I startled when you yelled, turning my body to dive out of the booth. It would have missed me completely if I'd been sitting still."

"You're delusional. "

"Come on. Who would be after me?"

"You were talking to Meg earlier. I don't know...let me think...the CIA? You told her you were helping me, didn't you?"

The idea that Meg would betray her made her laugh. "I didn't say anything about you. The swans have no reason to kill me, Tommy. You're the one with a target on your back."

After that, he fell silent, and she continued to maneuver him through the city, keeping a close eye on anyone who appeared to be following them. It was hard not to let down her guard when she saw no one who fit the bill and no other shots rang out. Taking out her phone, she called a ride service as they continued to walk. Three blocks east, they met the driver, who dropped them a hundred yards from her apartment.

Her entire arm felt numb, and she had to grind her teeth against the pain. This was the first time she'd ever been shot, come to think of it. It wasn't an experience she wanted to repeat.

"Let me do surveillance before we go in," Tommy demanded.

"Hurry," she said. She needed pain relievers in the worst way.

He was gone for nearly five minutes, her staying out of sight in one of the public gardens that were few and far between in this part of the city. When he finally rejoined her, he looked grim. "We need to go."

"Someone's casing the place?"

He took her by the hand and began leading her away

at a fast clip. "I can't see anyone, but something's off. I can feel it in my gut."

Paranoia or true instinct? Her stomach fell. She really needed those pain meds and a bandage. Should she take the risk and go in anyway? "You're being paranoid again. I'm telling you, no one is after me. I don't know who the shooter is, but if she wanted us dead, she'd still be on our trail."

"We're not going into that building."

Stubborn SOB. She tugged her hand out of his. "I'm not running away because your gut says something's off. Everything about this is off. You're overreacting because we were shot at, and I get it. It's triggered your overprotectiveness, but there's no reason we can't..."

A van on the street slowed. The windows were tinted, and she couldn't see the driver. Tommy noticed it, too. He grabbed her by her uninjured arm and propelled her past the water fountain. "Move!" he barked.

The motor revved, the van speeding up. She didn't need to be told twice. Sprinting toward another of the busier streets that ran past her apartment building, she forgot the pain in her arm. Her chest squeezed with fear —dammit, this was precisely why she didn't do spy shit anymore. She wasn't cut out for getting shot and being on the run.

"My car..." she panted as they emerged onto the narrow sidewalk. Hoofing it around the city on foot was for the birds. "It's two blocks west."

When he saw she was leading them to a concrete

parking garage, he groaned. "It's too dangerous. We could get cornered in there."

"Fine." She didn't have the energy to argue. She waved him off. "Go your own way. It was nice knowing you."

"*Tessa*," he snapped in warning.

As she sprinted into the structure that reeked of wet concrete and motor oil, she fished her keys from her pocket. A moment of satisfaction hit when she heard him race up behind her.

A battered Honda pulled into the garage, but there was no sign of the van. Her legs shook as she raced up the stairs to the third level, pushing aside the dizziness creeping in.

Her older model, Dacia, waited for them. The car brand had the same name the Romans had given this area before it became the country of Romania. Dacias were popular, and her Sandero blended in with most vehicles on the road.

"I'll drive," Tommy said.

She tossed him the keys. "You know the streets well enough?"

"I've worked here for the past year." He slid into the driver's side as she climbed into the passenger side. "I can manage."

Good thing it was Sunday. She knew one place she could easily access and get cleaned up without attracting attention. "Head north," she told him.

He took directions well, but his mood didn't improve.

"If it wasn't Meg who sold you out, it must be Vasile and Sorina."

The skin of her arm burned as if on fire. "They didn't," she bit out. "They wouldn't. I have too much on them."

"It's the only thing that makes sense."

But it didn't—not to her. The couple had been her most reliable assets for the past three years.

Yet, there had to be a connection. What was it?

Tommy seemed to realize at the last minute where she was taking them. "You're kidding," he said, pulling into a parking space down the block.

Fear that she might not be able to walk that far ate at her. "Bring the keys," was all she said as she hauled herself out, dragging the backpack with her.

As she kept her spine ramrod straight and prayed they hadn't been followed since there was no way she could run again, she avoided the giant entry doors of the *Biblioteca Naţională a României* and led Tommy to the entrance marked 'Employees Only.'

While much of the library had been upgraded in recent years, this entrance only required a simple key to access. The security camera above the door no longer worked.

She took the keyring from Tommy, fingers trembling as she searched for the correct one. Goosebumps covered her body—she was so cold. The ground undulated like an ocean wave under her feet, and she dropped the ring, slamming a hand against the door to steady herself.

Tommy grabbed her good arm to keep her from falling. "I told you not to pass out on me." He scooped up the keys with his free hand. "Which one am I looking for?"

She wiped rain from her eyes and snatched it from him, finding the one she wanted. Teeth chattering, she held it up and he gently took it from her, using it to unlock the door.

Inside, the library's familiar hush welcomed her. The smell of leather-bound books, dried paper, and the lofty air of knowledge called to her. She'd always felt safe here. Now, she wondered if she would be able to save her job. If she continued on this road with Tommy, her reliable, risk-free life would be over.

The cavernous lobby was dimly lit, the security desk unstaffed. The faint smell of the janitor's lemon polish tickled her nose.

Tommy followed her up the broad steps to the third floor. Her haven. Each day, she came here and filed away the books that patrons checked out. She found incredible volumes in Romanian and English that sparked her curiosity, deepened her thought processes, and challenged her beliefs, reading them on her breaks and taking some of them home to stack next to her bed for late-night reading.

"Stay close," she murmured, allowing his hand to remain on her elbow. She was glad for it, her entire body shaking now. She bypassed her office and ducked into the employee lounge, locking the door behind them. The room was small but functional, with a battered couch, a mini fridge, and a sink.

"Sit down," he ordered.

Although the female in her balked at his gruffness, her legs wobbled so hard, she was happy to do so, sinking into the cushions with relief.

He snatched a dish towel from the counter and ran it under the faucet, ringing it out and bringing it to her. With a gentleness that surprised her, he helped her remove her coat. She hissed as the agony flared to life again. The room spun, and she unwillingly toppled sideways.

Tommy said, "Whoa, there. You're going into shock."

"I need...aspirin..." she said through her chattering teeth.

Once he got her upright, he removed his bloody handkerchief from her wound and stuck it in his pocket. Then he began cleaning her injury. "You need more than that."

She bit her lip to keep from crying out. It wasn't just the pain; it was the realization that they couldn't go back to her place. Her apartment had never been compromised before. It was her sanctuary. Dammit all to hell.

He rinsed out the towel. "Do you have a first aid kit in this place? You need stitches."

"It's just a scratch. No stitches."

"While it's not deep, there's a generous amount of tissue damage."

Her words came out clipped. "Behind the circulation desk, and a second is in the head librarian's office."

He used paper towels to form a compress and handed it to her. Then he checked the fridge and found a bottle of water. "Keep pressure on the wound and drink this. I'll be back in a minute."

"There are security cameras on both of those places," she warned before he could storm out. "You can't go anywhere near them."

He glanced over his shoulder when he got to the door. "Let me worry about that."

And then he was gone.

SIX

Disabling security cameras? He could do that in his sleep. Retrieving a first aid kit? Easy as pie.

Tightening the makeshift tourniquet above Tessa's arm and watching her jaw tighten? He wanted to rip someone to pieces for causing her so much pain.

Sweat gleamed on her forehead, and her usually piercing gaze was dull under the haze of pain and blood loss. She was fighting shock—he could see it in the way she gritted her chattering teeth. Her whole body trembled. Her chest heaved with shallow breaths. More than that, her lips kept forming arguments that she didn't have the strength to voice.

"Hold still," he said, keeping his voice as calm as possible. It was a calm he didn't feel. She was convinced the shooter had purposely tried to miss both of them, but he didn't believe that. Then there was the van.

It took everything he had to keep his finger steady as he threaded the needle with a surgeon's precision. He'd had to patch himself up more than once. The needle glinted under the dim lounge light, the sterile smell of alcohol filling the air between them.

"I am," Tessa shot back with a waver in her voice. She cleared her throat, seemingly annoyed that she was showing weakness.

"It's not every day you get shot and go into shock. It's okay to let me take care of you."

Even hurt, she didn't cut him any slack. "I take care of...myself. I have since I was...nine."

Jessie had once mentioned that she suspected Tessa had been abused, or at least neglected, growing up. When Jessie had pried, though, Tessa had refused to talk about it. Tommy wondered if she'd been in the UK's version of the system that he and his sister had suffered through. "I get it—you're as tough as they come."

He meant it sincerely, but he saw her eyes narrow, assuming he was being flippant. Her voice came out stronger this round. "Not tough. Resilient."

It was the same thing in his world, but anything he could say was meaningless in this moment. His actions mattered. He wiped away another trail of seeping blood and earned a curse from her. "I don't like this either," he told her. The gash was clean but ragged. "An inch to the right and you'd be missing more than your favorite jacket."

"I'm telling you, our shooter didn't mean to hit me."

Whatever. "This is going to sting."

"Just do it."

Her flinch as the antiseptic soaked into the gaping

injury was minimal, but her knuckles whitened where she gripped the edge of the table. "Ever been shot before?" he asked.

She shook her head, lips tight. Glancing away as he slipped the needle under one edge of the gash, she blinked hard. "I did a quality job on you," she ground out. "You better return the favor."

His injury was on the mend, thanks to her. He was grateful, but he was no sewer. "Can't guarantee anything."

Silence encircled them, nothing but the ticking of a clock on the wall breaking it as he focused on her delicate, pale skin. She'd downed the water, and he'd given her some oxycontin that he'd found in the head librarian's stash in her desk. Much stronger than aspirin, they seemed to be already relieving some of Tessa's pain. He had to make sure to keep her warm and hydrated, so she didn't lapse back into shock.

"You're sure about them?" he asked.

She read his mind. "Vasile and Sorina didn't sell us out."

"I don't trust—"

"But I do. They don't know you. They have no connection to the embassy riot or Hagar. None to Jessie or the swans or..."

The final stitch cut her off as she sucked in a breath. He trimmed the thread. "Or what?"

She blinked as if she'd been lost in thought and he'd interrupted. "What?"

The shock was still taking its toll. "If not Vasile and Sorina, who then? You said it was a woman."

"I only got a quick glance, but her size, her posture... I'm fairly certain our shooter is female."

He wouldn't rule it out. "Why would she fire at us but not mean to hit us? It doesn't make sense."

"I don't know." Again, she paused, seemingly lost in thought. "To warn us off? Chase us away?" She shrugged, examining his handiwork. "She must have had a reason."

He wiped his hands and shoved the kit aside. Searching cabinets, he found a mug and tea bags. He shoved the water-filled mug in the microwave and zapped it. "This whole thing has gone to hell, and I haven't even started on my quest to retrace Jessie's footsteps before Vienna. I should leave you here. You're in danger because of me."

"Stop it." Her tone was filled with rebuke. "We're alive, and you're not going on alone. We need your passport, and then we're heading for Arizona."

The microwave dinged, and he dunked a bag into the steaming liquid. "You're going back to the tourist shop? Are you nuts?"

"Stop being dramatic. Vasile will do anything to get his money, including bringing the papers to me."

He helped her into her jacket and added his own, like a blanket over her shoulders. She sighed. "You're going to meet him in public?"

Accepting the tea, she sipped. "A dead drop. He's done them for me before."

"I thought you didn't do *spy shit*," he said, slipping a challenging note into his voice.

She made a rude gesture, and to his surprise, he laughed. It felt good, too.

He drew her to the couch with her cup and put an arm around her. She quirked a brow at him. "We need to warm you up to offset the shock."

Placated, she snuggled against him. The scent of her shampoo filled his nose, and he kept his breathing even, ignoring the way his pulse skipped at her nearness.

She laid her head on his shoulder, and his intentions went out the door. He swallowed hard. Inhaled deeply. Rubbed her good arm with gentle, soothing strokes.

Color returned to her cheeks. Her rapid breathing slowed. She finished the tea. "I need to hit the restroom before we go," she said.

Her voice sounded husky, sexy. He smiled to himself, realizing he was having the same effect on her as she was on him. "Of course," he said, but neither of them moved.

She set the empty cup aside and pressed her hand against his chest. Her pretty eyes, framed by thick lashes, met his. "I appreciate the stitches."

"Just returning the favor."

The way she stared at him made his already jumpy pulse kick harder. "You're a hero in my eyes, you know."

He wasn't sure what to say to that. "Why?"

"Uncovering this plot and going after those responsible is extremely brave."

Brave or stupid? He didn't care as long as she kept looking at him like that. "I'm not a hero, T."

She ran a finger down his cheek. "In my book, you are. Better get used to it."

Heroes ended up on pedestals. He wanted no part of that. "I'm just trying to do the right thing."

Her gaze settled on his lips. She was so close, so... alive. "Me, too." She ran a thumb over his bottom lip, and he couldn't breathe. She touched her lips to his. "Thank you."

That oxy was messing with her. With him. The drugs —and maybe the brush with death—had combined into this flirty cocktail.

All the blood had drained from his brain. "For what?"

"For reminding me who I am."

He was about to ask who exactly that was, but she stood, shedding his jacket and collecting the bloody paper towels. She shoved them into an interior jacket pocket, grabbed the rest of the pills he'd stolen, and pocketed them, too.

Still stunned by the kiss, he sat there like an idiot, watching her pull out her phone and type a text before she flicked her gaze to him. "Are you just going to sit there?"

He gave her arm a pointed look. "You really think you're up for this?" He needed to diffuse the live wire of attraction between them. "If you collapse, I'm not carrying you."

That did the trick. She huffed a chuckle. "If I collapse, you get that passport and head to Arizona. I want your promise that you won't let anything stop you from this mission."

Such determination. Such conviction. It mirrored his own. "I promise."

By the time they exited the library, the sun had dipped below the horizon. This section of the city was quiet; the street bathed in the yellow glow of street lights. Tessa seemed stable as they stepped into the night. He drove again, and she directed him to the dead drop site. On the way out of the library, she'd lifted a manila envelope and now tucked paper bills into it.

The dead drop location wasn't far from the tourist shop. They left the car behind and kept to the side streets, moving in the shadows.

Every sound made him jump. At one point, he grabbed her shoulder and pulled her into an alcove. "Wait," he whispered in her ear.

She gave a slight shudder but held still. He could almost hear her heart pounding as a car slowly drove down the street. The headlights moved past them without pause, but tension hung in the air.

It wasn't the van. "False alarm," he said, releasing her reluctantly.

They resumed their cautious trek until the shop came into view. Turning in the opposite direction, they found a bus stop, and Tessa slipped the manila envelope under the seat.

"You sure he'll come?" Tommy asked.

"Just watch."

Sorina walked down the sidewalk with a neutral expression, talking on her cell phone in Romanian. She sat on the bench, tucking a large tote between her feet and leaning forward, continuing her conversation.

Tommy kept a close eye on their surroundings. A single person crossed the street farther down the block, but he was busy texting and didn't look their way. Sorina deftly retrieved the envelope and stuck it in her bag. In the next second, she placed a matching one in the same spot under the bench.

The bus barreled down the street and stopped in front of her. Still talking on her phone, she picked up her bag and boarded. They waited an additional minute before Tessa went to grab the envelope.

Tommy stopped her. "Let me."

He didn't even try for subterfuge. He simply walked up, ripped the envelope from its hiding spot, and jammed it inside his coat, jogging back to her.

He took her by the hand and hustled her to her car.

SEVEN

The safe house was a nondescript structure in a quiet corner of a rundown neighborhood outside the city.

It looked like any other weathered building in this part of town—a faded façade with crumbling bricks and shutters half open. Tommy eyed it through the windshield, shooting Tessa a you-can't-be-serious look.

"I know, I know," she said. "It's ugly and looks like a fire trap, but trust me, it's safe."

He shut off the car engine. "You have two places."

A statement, but the question behind it was obvious. She was so, so tired, but she hid it behind irritation. "This one is for emergencies only."

She'd made Tommy drive around for an hour, waiting for night to fall, before directing him here. She exited the car and stomped up the sidewalk, closely monitoring the yard and neighboring lots.

It was all she could do to put one foot in front of the other, but she dug deep for the well of willpower buried under the layers of her resolute decision. Whether she wanted to be or not, she was in this now one hundred percent. There was no longer a way to go back, to return to her peaceful life. Whoever had shot her knew she was helping Tommy. That meant there was no path but the one forward.

She had to see this to the end.

He was nearly soundless as he trailed behind her. She wondered who'd trained him at The Farm. Why he'd chosen to become a counterterrorism analyst rather than an operative performing field missions like the swans? Or a hacker like Del. Maybe he hated undercover work like her.

Yet, he seemed efficient at it. Had Flynn recruited him to be a spy among spies? Had Tommy confessed it to Jessie--that he'd been running operations without any of them knowing?

Undercover work wasn't something that clicked with everyone. Deep undercover work was a beast of its own.

Nor did just anyone, no matter how intelligent or skilled, have the talent for spying. It was a rare breed who embodied the imagination, abilities, and strategic thinking that made them good at such work.

Tessa flicked on the lights as they entered the house through the back door. She stopped in the tiny mudroom to reset the security system, wincing as she shrugged off her jacket. She dropped that and the backpack on a hook before going to the kitchen and filling the coffee pot with water.

"Why the hell didn't we come here first?" Tommy

asked, kicking off his shoes before sidling up beside her and taking over with the coffee preparations.

She sagged into a chair. "Because I didn't know if we were being followed. This is my safe house. It hasn't been compromised—yet. I want to keep it that way."

Tommy threw grounds into the coffee maker and flipped the machine on. "If it wasn't Vasile and Sorina who gave us up, someone followed me to your apartment." He turned to face her. "But I've been staying there for the past week, and nobody disturbed us. Why wait to shoot at us until we were at the café? They had plenty of opportunities before then."

Another piece of this puzzle that made no sense to her. "If they'd wanted us dead, they would've come for us in my apartment. To shoot at us in public and not continue to follow us and get the job done means they were making a statement. They took a risk to do it like that, and now we know they're after us. That forces us to be even more covert. A professional assassin would never do that. First of all, they wouldn't miss. Secondly, they would only do it publicly if there was no alternative." She rubbed her face with both hands and propped her elbows on the tiny table. She needed caffeine or a very long nap. "It's just...sloppy."

He paced the floor, the smell of the brewing coffee filling the air as he stripped off the silicone pieces she'd added to his face. "The Russians are never sloppy."

"Neither is the CIA." She knew he still suspected Meg or Flynn might be behind it. "Which means it points to a new player in this game. Any thoughts on who?"

He shook his head, tossed the brow and cheekbone ridges on the table, and rummaged for mugs in the cabinet. "You said it was a woman."

She rubbed her eyes. At this point, she wasn't sure about anything. "It could have been a slender male."

He handed her a mug of steaming liquid and sat at the end of the table, kicking back. "What's next?"

She sipped slowly, the coffee too hot but soothing, nevertheless. "Shower, eat, and plan for tomorrow." She gestured behind them. "Bathroom is down the hall. Meg and Declan broke the bed when they were here, but I salvaged it. Go get cleaned up."

He watched her with those dark, sullen eyes over the rim of his cup. "What about you?"

"I want to look at your new documents."

She started to get up, but he stopped her with a hand. Without a word, he retrieved the envelope from his jacket and slid it onto the table in front of her. He resumed his seat, watching as she unpacked the items, scrutinizing each one thoroughly before handing it to him.

After his own careful inspection, he set the driver's license and passport down and leaned back. "He does good work."

She felt a slight sense of satisfaction. "That's why I use him."

The question in his eyes suggested he wanted to know how often she'd gone to Vasile and for whom, but he didn't ask. "What's the plan for tomorrow? If someone is after us, shouldn't we get out tonight?"

"Panicking only leads to making poor decisions. I need to check train schedules and flights. Once I figure out plan A, I'll develop plans B and C."

Deliberate, tactical. Declan would be proud. She waited for Tommy to argue, but all he did was give a sharp nod. "Fine, but you're showering first."

Her protests fell on deaf ears as he coerced her out of the chair and onto her feet. Dizziness assailed her, and she had to grab his arm to keep from knocking into the table.

"Easy there, champ." He placed a hand on her lower back, giving her a moment to blink away the vertigo before he led her through the living room. Although the room didn't swim, her legs were shaky. His grip was firm, his presence comforting. "It's my fault, you know. "

"Huh?"

"You never would've been shot if it weren't for me."

Down the hallway they went, his hand never leaving her as he used his elbow to flick on more lights. "I chose to help you. You didn't force me to." Why did she feel the need to argue with him? To relieve his guilt? "I don't do complexes, so let it go."

They reached the bathroom adjacent to the single bedroom. He took in everything, from the shabby bedspread to the small armoire and chest of drawers.

She shrugged. "It's a safe house, not a five-star hotel."

He released her in the bathroom. "I'll grab you some clean clothes."

"I can do it," she insisted.

Again, when she expected him to argue, he didn't. He was such a conundrum. "I'll dig up some food. If you get in a jam, holler."

He left her standing there, and she was both relieved and disappointed.

The hot water stung against her wound, but she gritted her teeth and scrubbed away the dried blood. By the time she emerged, steam curling around her like a phantom, she felt marginally more human.

And found a pile of clean clothes waiting for her on the vanity. He'd even refilled her coffee mug.

No arguing, but defying her anyway.

She wiped condensation from the mirror and grimaced at her reflection. She looked like hell.

Felt like it, too.

She found him in the kitchen, a spread of food on the table. He'd found her hidden laptop—he was definitely more operative than analyst—and was scanning the screen. "Why are we taking a train?"

"To get to the nearest airport. There, we'll fly to London and grab a flight to the US. We travel as strangers."

When he glanced up, his assessment of her reminded her of the same scrutiny he'd applied to the passport and driver's license. It started with her wet hair that she piled on top of her head, then her tank top, his gaze like a brand raking over her collarbone, her shoulders, down her arms.

His focus snagged momentarily on her stitches before

drifting to the snug-fitting yoga pants and down to her bare feet.

Everywhere his eyes went, a fire lit inside of her. Not like the ache in her arm from the bullet, but from something very female. The part of her that was exceptionally lonely.

He took a moment to refocus on her face and seemed to need time to remember the gist of their conversation before he replied. "Why not go straight to the States?"

"Two reasons." She sunk into a chair and helped herself to crackers and dried fruit. "First, I want to make sure your passport works without raising any red flags. Secondly, we'll draw less attention flying into the United States from the UK than from here."

He rested his elbows on the table, continuing to study her. "What if the passport pings something?"

"That's what plans B and C are for."

"Which you're going to let me in on, right?"

She stuffed her face and chewed, avoiding his eyes. She didn't want to talk about plans at the moment. She wanted to force him to the bedroom to undress him. "Sure," she said around a mouthful.

"You've got it all figured out, huh?"

Like before, his voice held a trace of challenge, and she glanced up to see him smiling at her. That smile... *damn.* The spot between her legs tingled, and it was everything she could do not to push him away from the table and climb into his lap. "Not everything," she told him. *I don't have you and me figured out yet.* "But I'm working on it."

He asked for details. She didn't give any. "You're up for a shower."

HER BODY BETRAYED her long before she admitted she needed rest. The adrenaline had worn off, leaving her limbs heavy and her mind foggy, even after the caffeine and the food.

Or maybe she was simply running away from her feelings. She tended to feel far too uncomfortable and exceptionally awkward around him.

However, she stayed at the kitchen table even after Tommy went to shower. It was better that she didn't get too close to that door—in her state, she might do something stupid and walk right in.

What if she did? What if she stripped off her clothes and climbed into the shower with him, only to find he didn't want her?

The horror of that scenario kept her seated and checking flights.

Eventually, her eyes drooped, and she laid her head on the table. Just for a minute—when she heard the shower shut off, she would perk back up and pretend to be as lively as...

She fell asleep. The next thing she knew, Tommy lifted her from the chair and carried her to bed. He smelled and felt so good. She liked his arms around her and enjoyed the gentleness with which he laid her on the bed and covered her with the blanket.

She made noises of protest, but he patted her shoulder. "Get some sleep. You're safe. "

She drifted off in dreams of strong arms and dark eyes.

Morning light filtered through the curtains when she stirred next. Her arm throbbed dully, but it was the familiar warmth beside her that made her ease deeper into the sheets.

Tommy's arm draped loosely over her waist, his breathing slow and steady.

For a moment, she didn't move, her mind scrambling to piece together how she'd gone from the kitchen to the bed—and why he was here with her. Then the memories flooded back, all except the part where he'd slipped in beside her.

They'd shared the same bed for nearly a week, but this felt different.

Her breath caught as he shifted, his eyes fluttering open. "Morning," he said, his voice thick and rough from sleep.

By the hardness pressing against her thigh, his voice wasn't the only thing that was thick. What would he do if she wrapped a hand around his erection and squeezed it?

He stared at her, one corner of his mouth quirking. "You all right?"

"What?"

"You seem surprised to see me."

"I, uh..." *Get it together, Tess!* "I'm fine." She nodded vigorously. Was she trying to convince him or herself?

A finger traced her jawline. "Good. You were shaking

during the night. I was worried you were going into shock again."

Worried. Like a friend would be. Of course. She pushed his arm away and sat up, swinging her legs over the edge of the mattress. The room didn't tilt. That was good. "Probably just a bad dream."

She started to rise, but he slid two fingers into her waistband and stopped her. She glanced over her shoulder.

He sat up, drawing her close. A hand slid from her wrist to her elbow. "Let me see."

The way his eyes locked on hers made her feel vulnerable. As if he were asking to see more than her injured arm. As he shifted to sit next to her, his touch was warm and gentle, his face only an inch from hers as he began to peel the bandage off her stitches.

He smelled like sleep and soap. His bare chest and his own recovering injury were on full display, tempting her to run her fingers over each peak and crevice.

As the latex gave way, revealing her red and sore skin, it felt as though he was uncovering more than just her wound. It was as if he were peeling away a layer of her shield.

"I'm fine," she repeated, the words coming out too soft and breathy to be believable. "It's fine."

His gaze rose to hers, holding it. "It's okay if you're not."

The buttress she'd built around her emotions began to tremble. She tried to pull away, but he held her by the wrist. Not forcefully, but securely, as if suspecting something inside her was about to break.

She wanted to lean into that, to him. To let him hold her up, steady her. For the first time in her life, she wanted someone to tell her it would all be okay.

Even if it was a lie.

The old panic that she hadn't allowed herself to feel since she was nine began to bubble right under her breastbone. Her throat tightened, and her lungs wouldn't fill. She searched for something to say. Anything. She had to get away from him. Away from his touch, those eyes that peered into her soul.

"Please," was all that came out. Her lips trembled, and her eyes filled with tears. Her internal buttress shook as if experiencing an earthquake. "I...I can't."

Can't what? She wasn't even sure what that meant.

His lips quirked. "I know." He replaced the bandage and let his fingers trace its outline. "Not yet," he continued. "But you will." He leaned his forehead against hers. "And I'll be here when you do."

EIGHT

Tommy sat on the edge of the bed, his hands braced on his knees, trying to ignore the tangle of emotions rolling through him. The early morning light seeped through the cracked blinds, painting stripes across the modest bedroom. Tessa had moved back and now sat cross-legged on the bed as if purposely putting a barrier between them.

"I can go on my own," he said. "You can return to your life."

She didn't reply for a long moment, sizing him up, a slight crease forming between her brows. It was both endearing and troubling. He wanted to brush it away, but he knew better than to touch her again right now. "You haven't said anything about your injury." She pointed to his wound several days further along in the healing process than hers.

It was still sore, and after their activity yesterday, it was aggravating him. Because of it, he'd had trouble getting comfortable during the night, but he'd kept close to her anyway. "Stitches are holding fine," he said. "It looks like we'll both live."

She gave a laugh, more of an exhale than anything genuine. "I'll be the judge of that." She wiggled her fingers at him. "Let me see."

He stood and turned so that his injured side faced her. Her fingers brushed against his skin, and he tried not to catch his breath. Not because it hurt but because he desired so much more. He wanted her warm, gentle fingers to explore beyond his wound.

And his morning erection came to full attention, bobbing under his waistband.

For an embarrassing heartbeat, neither of them moved or said anything. He snuck a peek at her and saw her blatant appraisal. When she caught him looking, she began examining her work again.

Doing the most challenging thing of his life, he backed away from her hand and spun around.

"It's okay," she said with a teasing note. "I know how the male body works, and I know that happy little guy has nothing to do with me."

He whirled back around. "*Little?*"

She grinned and unfolded her legs. Long, beautiful legs. Standing before him, she put her hands on her hips, lifting her chin and challenge. "Morning erections are nothing to be embarrassed about."

"*I'm* not embarrassed. I thought you were. I was trying to be respectful."

The grin widened. His gaze dropped to her mouth.

He wanted to kiss her. He *could* kiss her. If that smile meant anything, it seemed she might welcome it.

Just as he was about to, the smile fell from her face, and her eyes darkened. She took a step back, stopping him cold.

She was scared.

Not of him, but of whatever was stirring between them. It was her turn to shift away, suddenly avoiding his gaze.

He reached for her. "Tessa..."

She skirted by him and his erection, avoiding his fingers. "I'm going to make coffee," she said, her tone clipped now.

Letting his hand fall to his side, he released an exasperated sigh. His erection deflated, and he ran a hand through his hair. He'd blown it. Whatever chance he might've had to break through the wall she kept around herself had vanished.

After cleaning up and getting dressed, he found the smell of coffee filling the small kitchen as he stepped inside. Tessa was at the counter, pouring it into two mismatched mugs. "Breakfast of champions," she said, sliding a mug across the counter to him.

He didn't know what to say about what had happened in the bedroom. Would his feeble attempts at an apology only make things worse? "Thanks," he muttered. He sipped, and the bitterness of the strong coffee matched the acid in his stomach.

They ate in silence, sharing a can of fruit and a sleeve of crackers scavenged from the pantry. He watched her from the corner of his eye, noting the way her fingers fidgeted with her napkin, her focus on everything but him.

"Didn't peg you for someone who runs from her feelings," he said, breaking the silence.

Her fingers stilled, and she arched a brow. "Excuse me?"

"Seems like you've been pushing everyone away since Jessie's death. Maybe before that, too. I'm curious why."

She gave a nonchalant shrug, but her thin lips told him it was forced. "There's nothing to tell."

"Sure, there is." He eased back in the chair, going for nonchalant himself. He sipped his coffee and didn't push for a minute as he used his fork to fish out another piece of the awful fruit. He chewed slowly, giving her time. "We all have a story."

Her eyes challenged him. "What's yours, then? You don't seem like the relationship type."

Ah. Was that why she didn't want to get involved with him? Not only was she afraid to let someone in, she feared he wasn't the type to stick around. If she did fall for him...

At least he had something to work with now.

He smiled faintly, letting her know he recognized the deflection for what it was. "All right. I'll go first."

He refilled their cups and grabbed another cracker. It wasn't easy to talk about any of this, and he waited for the old resistance to fill his chest and make his throat tight. When he looked at her, sitting there, totally open and ready to listen, however, neither happened.

"Our parents were killed in an accident. That's how Jessie and I ended up in the system." He gave her a few details, not sugarcoating it, but didn't downplay the chaos or the fear, either. "She was twelve. I was ten."

"You had your world completely upended."

He resumed his seat, setting the coffee pot on the cracked linoleum table between them. "I was lucky. Jessie was tough. She did everything she could to keep us together. Even when they stuck her in a foster home halfway across town, she snuck out every night and ran sixteen blocks to check on me. I was with a different family. Eventually, she got caught climbing through my window and got sent to a home even farther away." He chuckled to himself, the memories coming back in full force. "That didn't stop her."

Tessa's features softened enough to make him think he'd struck a chord. "I'm not surprised."

"She was amazing," he said. "She made sure I always knew I wasn't alone."

For a moment, the only sound was the faint hum of the refrigerator. Tessa ate the final piece of fruit from the can and sipped her coffee. Tommy glanced out the window, wondering if his confession made any difference in gaining her trust.

She rose, throwing the plastic sleeve from the crackers away and rinsing the can in the sink. Guess that was his answer.

He wanted to ask about their itinerary for the day,

but his heart wasn't in it. Going on the run with her to trace Jessie's steps had seemed exciting and necessary yesterday. Today, he wasn't sure. All he could think about was Tessa.

She took her coffee and walked out of the kitchen. His heart sank.

He tried to find the energy to get up and move, but what was there to do? Throwing his clothes into his backpack would take all of a minute.

When she returned, she'd changed clothes and put on makeup. A lot of makeup. She laid her cell phone on the table and sat, bracing her hands on the tabletop and staring a hole in it.

"My stepdad was a drunk," she said, her tone flat. "Mean, too. He beat my mom on the regular. One night, they got into a bad one. Things got out of hand, and he—" she paused, drawing in a deep breath that seemed to come all the way up from her toes. "He killed her. Right in front of me. I saw the light leave her eyes."

Tommy's chest went tighter than a ripcord.

"He went to prison, but he was a consultant for the Agency, and they covered up a lot of his shit."

"He was a spy?"

"*Consultant*," she repeated, making air quotes. "He was only charged with manslaughter and was placed in a special lockup to keep him from talking about the secrets he knew. I got shipped off to live with my aunt in London. She wasn't cruel, but she didn't want me there. Made that clear every chance she got. I never met my grandparents." Her gaze drifted to the window. "I couldn't wait to get out on my own. Been taking care of myself ever since."

He suspected she'd been caring for herself since before her mother died. He wanted to comfort her, but what was there to say? She would only push him away, thinking it was pity. "Jessie said you were royalty or some shit."

Her chuckle was dry and devoid of emotion. "Brushing cousins on my mom's side. She came from a well-off British family with lands and titles. I'm officially a Lady, the daughter of a British earl and a countess, but it means nothing. My father died when I was a baby, and once my mother remarried an American, her family disowned her. And me."

"That's why you don't let anyone in, right? You lost both your parents and your extended family, and then you took a chance with Jessie, and she died. Now, you won't risk it."

"Relationships are bad for my heart."

"You don't want to need anyone because needing them makes you vulnerable. They can let you down."

Her eyes swung to him. "They don't simply let me down. They *die*."

He nodded. Said nothing.

After a moment, her shoulders slumped, and she let out a soft, bitter laugh. "Maybe, Mr. Therapist, I just don't like people."

"You like me."

The corner of her mouth twitched. "Don't push it."

He raised his hands in surrender. "Like a good therapist, I'm simply stating facts. Holding up a mirror so you can see yourself."

She was about to retort when her phone rang. The smile on her face disappeared. "It's Meg."

Shit.

Tessa chewed her bottom lip as if debating whether to answer. Then she punched the screen and put the call on speaker. "Yes?"

"Good morning to you, too," Meg answered. "Any news?"

Tessa met Tommy's gaze. He held his breath for a heartbeat, seeing the struggle behind her eyes. She was weighing outcomes, considering whether to give him up. She dropped her attention back to the phone. "Nothing new. Has Del decoded more of the information?"

Damn, she was good at deflection. Tommy held his breath again, for a different reason this time.

"The USB had a virus that was triggered once he got to the second level. It completely wiped the drive. We have no idea now what else Tommy had on it."

He let out the breath he was holding.

Tessa eyed him suspiciously. "He's smart."

The admiration in her tone and her eyes made his chest swell. He tried not to show it.

"Smart, yes, but what's he up to? Look, Dec and I are flying there later today." Meg rattled off the flight details. "Pick us up at the airport at seven, okay?"

Tessa blanched and ran a finger along the edge of the phone. "I'm afraid I can't do that."

"Tessa, come on. We need you on the swans. You have to help us find Tommy."

Again, Tessa hesitated. Tommy wasn't sure if she was coming up with an excuse to avoid Meg and Declan, or if she was about to give him up.

"I wish I could," she said. "I won't be here when you arrive."

He still didn't dare to breathe. Meg made an exasperated sound in the back of her throat. "Where are you going? "

"To London and then Arizona." Tommy winced at the fact she shared even that much. "Visiting friends."

"You don't have friends."

Tessa stuck her tongue out at the phone. He wasn't the only one stating facts this morning. "You're welcome to use my place as your home base," Tessa said, "but I won't be there for a while."

Declan came on the line. Meg must've had the conversation on speakerphone as well. "Tessa, I know you don't want to be involved in this, but your country needs you," he said. "We're running out of time, and if we don't find Tommy and figure out what all he uncovered about the EMP attacks, a lot of people will get hurt. Can't you postpone your visit?"

"No, Dec, I can't, and if Tommy knows what's happening, I'm sure he's working to stop it, just like you are." Her intense eyes zeroed in on him. "The swans should quit worrying about his whereabouts and focus on stopping the attacks. Now, like I said, you're welcome to stay at my place. It's a mess, but better than nothing. Other than that, I can't help you. Good luck."

She punched the disconnect button and chewed her bottom lip again. "That was stupid."

He was so thankful she hadn't betrayed him, he didn't understand. "What?"

"Offering them my place. They'll realize I had company."

"And that's rare for you."

She narrowed her eyes. "Rare, but not unheard of. I happen to be good at ending up with the wrong guy in my bed on occasion. If they suspect I had a visitor, hopefully, they don't realize it was you."

Wrong guy in her bed. Was that how she saw him?

She stood. "Let's go. The train leaves in two hours."

"We've got plenty of time."

"I need to make a stop first."

"Where?"

"You'll see."

Again, she was unwilling to share more than a few details. It frustrated him, but what could he do? He'd agreed to let her be in charge.

They packed and were ready to leave in less than ten minutes. He paused at the back door, catching her arm gently. She tensed but didn't pull away. "Thanks," he said.

"For what?"

It was a flippant, automatic response.

"For all this, but particularly about sharing what happened to your family. To you."

She blinked, then nodded once.

Then, shocking him, she rose on her toes and kissed his cheek. Her lips brush the corner of his mouth.

She turned and walked out into the morning drizzle before he could react and pull her into his arms.

He understood now—why she kept people at arm's length. Why she was so determined to be in charge of everything and do things her way.

You don't have to anymore, he vowed.

Following her, he swore to himself to make sure she never felt abandoned or alone again. He'd be there for her and make sure she knew what it felt like to be loved and taken care of.

Before this was all over with, he'd break through those damn walls of hers, and he wouldn't stop until she let him in.

NINE

The heavy glass doors of the bank closed behind Tessa with a muted thud, leaving the bustling noise of the street muffled behind her.

Inside, the scent of polished wood and faintly acrid toner filled the air. She didn't stop her stride, keeping her sunglasses on as she approached the receptionist with measured confidence. Everything about her said *ordinary*. She was simply another client visiting her safe deposit box.

Down the block, Tommy sat in her car, petulant. She'd insisted he stay behind. She didn't want him anywhere near the bank.

Going through the standard steps required to access the box, she slipped her ID across the desk to the clerk and signed off on a digital pad. Here, she used her real name and didn't need to avoid the cameras that tracked her every movement, although it was second nature to turn her head away from their probing scanners.

Inside the tiny room next to the vault, the generous-sized metal box before her, she took a moment to breathe. This was it—the safety net she'd created years ago but had prayed she never need.

Now, she did.

The first thing that greeted her inside was a collection of miscellaneous contracts and papers that all regular, upstanding citizens possessed. She removed them and the fake bottom she'd installed and examined what lay underneath.

Multiple aliases, passports, documents, and individual bags labeled with names corresponding to those fake IDs were tucked neatly in the metal confines. Each bag was meticulously organized and tailored to a specific alias.

She thumbed through the passports, settling on one for Kaitlyn Brown. A nondescript American who traveled in Europe for an international office supply company. Boring and ordinary. The bag corresponding to Kaitlyn had a makeup kit, hair dye, and a carefully folded microfiber outfit. It was everything she needed to transform herself into the woman on the passport.

She grabbed a second, smaller bundle of cash—euros, dollars, and a few denominations she wouldn't need but took anyway. You just never knew who you had to bribe and what currency they preferred.

Her Sig Sauer fit perfectly in the space left behind. She hated being without it, but it was better not to attempt to take it through airport security. Even if she dismantled it and put the pieces into CIA-approved containers that mimicked everyday items, it would be two chancy. And while all of her aliases had a permit to carry, Kaitlyn Brown didn't seem the type.

Inventorying everything one last time, she placed the items into her backpack and closed the box with a soft click. A minute later, she was outside and found Tommy leaning on the side of the car, waiting for her. Even as he spotted her, he kept scanning the street, the buildings, the alleys. Nothing escaped his notice.

"All good?" he asked.

She nodded and crooked her finger in a gesture for him to follow. Leaving the car, she led him down several busy streets to a French boutique four blocks from the bank.

The shop was exactly as she remembered it: opulent, intimidating, and discrete. The interior sparkled with glass cases displaying overpriced jewelry and racks of clothing better suited for runways than real life.

Posh carpeting silenced their footsteps, and Tommy murmured in her ear, "What are we doing here?"

"You'll see."

A female clerk who looked like she could walk one of those runways approached with a warm smile. The gold choker around her neck probably cost more than the money Tessa had secured in her backpack. She greeted them in Romanian, then English. "May I help you?"

"Is Miriam working?" Tessa asked.

The woman's smile faltered. "I'm so sorry. Miriam is no longer employed here. May I be of assistance?"

That was disappointing. Tessa slipped a crisp, folded

bill out of her pocket and made sure to catch the woman's eye with it. "What I need is a few minutes alone with my husband in your dressing room. I'll make it worth your while."

The clerk's gaze went between her and Tommy, a sly smile passing over her features this time. There didn't appear to be anyone else in the shop, and she probably needed to make her quota for the day. Hard to do if you didn't have clientele. "Of course. Perhaps I could show you the latest Miro Hasaki? You're a size thirty-eight? Thirty-nine?"

The European dress sizes translated to roughly a size six or seven. A bit small for her, but it didn't matter. "Thirty-nine will do."

The clerk grabbed an atrocious orange and green dress from one of the displays and gestured for them to follow. She then hung the dress on the back of the changing room door, gave Tessa a knowing wink, and said, "I hope you find it to your satisfaction."

Tessa locked the door behind her, her pulse racing from the risk she was taking. The room was small yet luxurious, featuring a bench, plush carpet, and peacock wallpaper. It included a sink beneath a large gilded mirror and a discreet water closet.

She dumped the contents of the Kaitlyn Brown bag on the counter and handed Tommy a smaller one filled with his silicone prosthetics and adhesive. "You're up," she said.

He groaned, opening the bag like it contained live snakes. "I have to do it myself?"

"Out of everything you've dealt with in the past year, you're going to complain about this?"

She slipped out of her jacket and flipped through her materials. Working efficiently, she shampooed the dye into her hair, making it more auburn. Next came contacts that matched that tone. She fattened her nose and thinned her lips.

Tommy seemed more fascinated with watching her in the mirror than transforming his features. All she had left to do was switch out her clothes, and he hadn't even done his cheekbones. He held a brow piece in one hand and the adhesive in the other, squinting at them like they were puzzle pieces.

Tessa grabbed the forms, motioning for him to sit on the counter. "Just... Sit still."

He hesitated but obeyed, grunting as he hoisted himself up. She stepped between his knees, her focus narrowing as she pressed the brow piece to his skin and smoothed the edges with practiced precision.

He was warm, and that heat seemed to radiate between them, making her acutely aware of how close they were. His hands shifted to her waist, casual-like.

Was this a test? After her quick thank you kiss this morning, was he pushing the boundaries to see how far he could go?

"Stop that," she snapped.

He dropped his hands to his thighs. "Sorry."

He didn't sound sorry in the least.

As she worked, her eyes kept straying to his lips. *Focus, Tessa.* She dabbed the adhesive with the brush, refusing to let her thoughts wander. He was staring at her but she refused to meet his gaze.

Where else could he look? she chided herself. *Of course, he's staring at you. You just became someone else.*

But it was more than that, and she knew it.

A part of her wanted him to put his hands back on her waist. Another inch, and she could brush her breast against his chest. Their breath mingled with their faces so close together, and all she had to do was lean closer to kiss him again.

"You've done this before," he said quietly. "I thought you weren't a spy."

"I've been trained in many things; this is one of them."

That focused gaze studying her made her stomach flutter. Her pulse ratcheted up again. "You're good at it."

She didn't trust herself to respond. His hand slid back to her hips, this time lingering, and she didn't demand he remove it. Her breath seemed stuck in her chest, and when she finally met his eyes, his expression was unreadable.

"Don't," she said, but the damage was done. Her resolve was crumbling faster than she could repair it.

"Tessa," he said just above a whisper.

A shiver ran through her, hearing her name spoken with such reverence. She stared at his lips, remembering their conversation at the kitchen table. How he'd looked at her like she mattered.

On impulse, so rare for her, she leaned in. Their lips met, and Tommy stilled.

Everything that had happened slid away. She wasn't thinking about anything now except how he felt against her.

He deepened the kiss, sliding off the counter, his arms wrapping around her. She let herself fall flush against him. The next thing she knew, she'd dropped the brush and adhesive, her back hitting the wall as he pinned her there.

She gasped, but it didn't stop him.

It didn't stop her, either.

She grabbed the locks of hair on top of his head with one hand and the back of his neck with the other. This is how she could forget. Forget all of it—Jessie's death, her mother's, all the others who had betrayed and left her.

This moment of freedom would come at a cost, but she didn't care. She wanted it, whatever risks it brought.

A knock sounded on the door. "Time is up," the clerk called. "You must leave now."

Tommy's hand pressed against the wall beside Tessa's head, his breath brushing her ear as he growled at the clerk, "Go. Away."

Reality came crashing back, unwanted. Tessa let her hands fall. "We can't stay," she whispered, her voice as shaky as her legs.

Tommy kissed her again, harder, his hand sliding down to her thighs. He lifted her effortlessly, and she instinctively wrapped her legs around his waist.

The bliss hit again, and all logic fled. His tongue found hers, and they danced together in that bliss.

The doorknob rattled, followed by a man's voice.

"Open up. I have called the police. They are on their way."

That got their attention. Tommy released her, and she mentally scolded herself as they both caught their breath.

Without a word, they scrambled to gather their things. Outside the door, the manager's voice rose in a mixture of French, Romanian, and furious English.

Tommy grabbed her hand, hauling her after him. They burst out of the dressing room and made a beeline for the exit. The manager's tirade followed them.

Outside on the sidewalk, Tessa's laughter bubbled up, uncontrollable and ridiculous, given their situation. But it was infectious, and she caught the grin spreading across Tommy's face as they ran from the boutique, like children playing a dangerous game.

TEN

Tessa really did look like a stranger.

Tommy sat on a bench near Platform Three, pretending to read the day's newspaper. Six feet away, she perched on another bench, legs crossed, her expression unreadable.

He preferred her natural hair color and couldn't get used to the change in her eyes. She insisted they act as strangers, and they had purchased tickets separately. Still, it was a challenge not to stare at her.

A man in a business suit dropped into the space next to her. He was balding, overweight, and sweating profusely. Tessa appeared not to notice, but Tommy bristled at the man's invasion of her personal space. The guy dabbed at his damp forehead and started making small talk.

Tommy eavesdropped as the guy's irritating, nasal voice grated on his nerves. Tessa barely acknowledged him, tapping away on her phone as if playing a computer game. Like so many assholes, the guy didn't take the hint, asking her what was so interesting as he glanced at her screen.

She didn't stop tapping and slid down the bench away from him.

Tommy knew she could take care of herself, but he still wanted to charge in and do something. Tell the guy to get lost or strike up a conversation with her in order to snub the asshole. It was everything he could do to stay planted in his seat.

The guy huffed and took out his own phone while Tessa peeked at Tommy, feeling his glare. She gave him a slight shake of her head and returned to her phone.

She'd changed into an ugly business suit, but even with the plain clothes and transformation of her naturally beautiful features, something about her caused people to do a double take. He doubted the chubby, balding asshole would be the only one to attempt to talk to her.

Tommy folded the paper and moved closer to a spot across from her. When she didn't look up, he cleared his throat. "Nice day for a train ride," he said, his voice just loud enough to carry to her.

Her lips pressed into a thin line, her eyes barely flicking up to meet his. She arched one brow, giving him a death glare. "Don't," she said under her breath, but he heard it.

Baldy must have, too. He glanced toward them, and Tommy looked away, studying one of the boards over the far gates. When the asshole went back to his own business, Tommy got up and sat on a bench behind Tessa.

With their backs to each other, he could speak more quietly and not draw attention while still teasing her. Snapping out the paper, he hid behind it as he said, "Don't what? Makes small talk? I'm just being friendly."

She didn't appreciate the teasing note in his voice, nor his risky behavior. "Stop it," she hissed. "What part of we're supposed to be strangers did you not understand?"

"Strangers make small talk. Just like the ahole down from you tried to."

Her exasperated sigh was music to his ears. "If you're trying to annoy me, it's working."

A snort escaped him before he could stop it. He wished he could see her face. The image of her laughing earlier, the sound of it as they fled the boutique, had stuck with him. It wasn't the same laugh he'd heard before—the dry, sarcastic kind she used like armor. This had been real, unguarded, and unexpected.

He wanted to hear it again.

"Pretend I'm flirting with you. Trying to impress you."

"You're going to have to try harder."

He chuckled again. "You're tough on a guy's ego, you know that?"

A group of loud travelers passed by, and he fell silent but lowered the paper to track them.

That's when he saw her.

Or thought he did.

It was just a flash—a face in the crowd, partially obscured by a scarf and a mass of people weaving toward the exit. But for a heartbeat, Tommy could've sworn it was Jessie. The tilt of her chin, the way she turned her head. The dark hair slipping from under her hood...

His breath caught and jammed in his throat.

Not Jessie. Jessie is dead. I buried her.

And yet... He stood, dropping the paper, his legs moving before his brain caught up. "Hey!" he shouted, shoving past the loud tourists gathered before him.

The figure turned a corner and disappeared into a stream of commuters. His heart pounded, and he forced his way through the crowds, scanning every face and figure for a glimpse of familiarity. Overhead, the drone of announcements faded into the background.

He couldn't help himself. "Jessie," he shouted. Heads turned, but none of them belonged to her. By the time he reached the end of the corridor, she had vanished.

He braced a hand on a pillar, sucking in a breath as the cold reality settled over him.

He was losing it. *My sister is dead. What is wrong with me?*

It hadn't been her at the cemetery after her burial. It hadn't been her in Bucharest before the embassy attack. His mind had been playing tricks on him then. It was now, too.

When he headed back to the bench, Tessa was striding down the corridor toward him, hands on her hips and a frown etched into her face. Both brows went up in question, and he shook his head, veering away from the crowd to stop with his back against one of the cement walls of the station. He needed it to brace himself.

She spoke under her breath. "What the hell was that?"

Tommy hesitated. She wouldn't let it go if he tried to brush her off, but he didn't have the energy to get into it. "Just my mind playing tricks on me."

The frown deepened. "Come on."

She led him outside, where the noise of the station faded. They moved to a section where smokers and those searching for rides hung out. She scanned him from head to toe, her eyes dissecting him as if she could see straight through to his brain. To all the secrets he was trying to keep from her. From himself. "Well?"

He ran a hand through his short hair, missing his longer locks, and exhaled hard. "It's stupid."

"Tell me anyway."

"I'd rather you didn't think I was delusional."

She moved so she was next to him, her back to the wall. People came and went, but they paid no attention to them. Still, she pulled out her phone and began tapping again. They were back to being strangers.

Was it because she was so stubborn or because he wouldn't confess the truth, and she was pissed?

Several minutes passed, and dozens of travelers swept by them. Announcements came over the loudspeakers. Tommy replayed what had happened in his mind. All the excuses he'd given himself before bubbled up hot and acidic to batter him: It was a trick of the light. It was just someone who looked similar to her. *You were thinking about her this morning, and so you brought her to life, transferring what you wish for onto someone else.*

"We should probably go back inside," he said.

She pushed off the wall and started to march past him.

Seeing her stiff posture, something inside him broke. "I thought I saw Jessie."

She stopped in mid-stride. "What?"

"It's happened three times in the past year." He whirled a finger around his temple. "Grief has screwed with my brain."

As if unsure how to respond, she backed herself against the wall again. Cigarette smoke lingered in the air. Disbelief tinged her voice. "Your sister, Jessie."

"After her funeral, I thought I saw her at the cemetery. One day before the embassy riot, I was heading to work, and I thought I saw her getting into a car with some guy. It always seems to happen in crowds. Talking about her this morning must have put her front and center in my mind, and then I saw someone who looked like her. That's all."

Her posture relaxed. "Perfectly normal. I still think I see my stepdad sometimes, and he's been dead for twenty years."

"Dead?"

"He was stabbed during a prison riot."

"Well, that sucks for both of us. Yet, hearing that you hallucinate a dead person, too, makes me feel somewhat better. Maybe I'm not losing my shit, after all."

She didn't argue. "There's a region of the brain called the right fusiform face area. It's strongly associated with processing the patterns of human facial features. It's why we can spot the faces of our loved ones in a sea of strangers. When it gets activated, it drowns out other conflicting messages. It's like a megaphone at a town hall meeting. Of course, like many other processes in human brains, it's easily tricked into making mistakes."

"Do I want to know how you know that?"

"Research. When I thought I saw my stepdad, I looked into it." She flicked a glance at him. "Is there anything else you're not telling me?"

He stiffened. She was like a lie detector—she always seemed to know when he was holding back.

"Tommy." Her voice was firm and too much like Jessie's had been when she was mothering him. "Whatever it is, spit it out."

The debate still raged inside him. It shouldn't be an issue, but it was. He knew she wasn't going to take it well. "Meg lied. About the virus on the USB."

Her body tensed. "Explain."

"There *is* a virus on it," he admitted. "But not one Del wouldn't catch. He's too good. I put it there so if morons like Hagar or his death squad got hold of the thing, they would trigger the virus, and it would delete all the information on the USB. It's well encrypted, but you never know. A computer genius like Del would have seen that virus and disabled it before it triggered."

"Why would Meg tell me differently?"

"Why do you think? "

"She has no reason to be dishonest."

"Doesn't she? Do you think she and Flynn trust you more than they do me?"

Her jaw tightened, but she said nothing.

"And before you ask," he continued, "no, I didn't put anything else dangerous on there. I added data I was gathering about the Russian investors, the computer company providing the sabotaged hardware, and some other stuff to the items Jessie had on it."

"What other stuff?"

There was no way he was telling her about the thread he'd been following. The evidence suggesting Jessie had ties to Hager and the Russian investors—and not because she was trying to expose them. He didn't believe it—couldn't believe it—but he hadn't been able to let it go. Not until he had proof either way.

Which was one of the reasons he needed to retrace Jessie's footsteps. "Nothing that's important at the moment."

"You're a terrible liar."

Before she could respond, the loudspeaker crackled, announcing their train's departure. "That's us," he said, straightening.

Tessa grabbed his arm. "We're not done with this discussion."

Of course, they weren't. "I know," he said, tugging out of her grip. "But it will have to wait."

They ran for the platform and were blocked by a group of tourists. He didn't want to be separated from Tessa, but she refused to let him guide her through the throng. He did his best to create a path for her, but people kept getting in the way.

Some guy knocked her backpack off. She shoved him

aside to retrieve it. By the time she'd done that and cut through the rest of the crowd, the final announcement for their train had gone out.

The platform they needed was on the other side of the station. Strangers or not, they both took off sprinting, dodging people, pets, and luggage, creating an obstacle course for them.

As they raced the last few steps, they received a stern look and a lecture from the conductor. "Cutting it close, aren't you?"

They handed him their tickets, and neither said a word.

He waved them inside and closed the doors right before the train took off.

ELEVEN

The train rocked gently as it glided over the tracks, the rhythmic clatter a dull background to Tessa's whirlwind thoughts. She sat near the window, several rows away from Tommy but within direct sight. Keeping her eyes on the passing scenery, she kept her demeanor neutral, almost bored. She was only a businesswoman on a commute, nothing more.

In this train section, seats faced each other, with tables in between. The two passengers across from her were busy on laptops and phones and paid little attention to her or anyone else. But she would feel Tommy's insistent stare.

Keeping her head turned toward the windows, she avoided his stare because he was going to blow their cover.

At least, that's what she told herself.

In reality, she kept her face averted from him and the others because of the doubts gnawing at her.

Tommy claimed he'd seen Jessie—not once but three times. Grief made people see ghosts where none existed. As she'd told him, she knew that firsthand.

But after what had happened, her brain kept insisting it wasn't a ghost.

It *had* been a woman who'd shot at them. She was sure of it. And the shooter had missed on purpose.

Was someone imitating Jessie to draw Tommy into some maddening game? Why? What purpose could there be in that? What tie could it have to the Russians and the EMPs, if anything?

She replayed the memory of Jessie's gruesome execution in her mind. It had most certainly been a living human being who'd had their head removed by Hagar's machete. Meg had confirmed that the remains had been verified as Jessica Mendoza by the CIA.

Meg, who'd been a complete and utter mess. Who'd been beaten and tortured for days before the rescue. Who'd been so traumatized over witnessing the brutal killing up close and personal that she'd been unable to speak for days. She'd been in a stupor for months. She'd quit the Agency over it.

Tessa needed to see the footage again. To zoom in on the woman's face. At first glance—on the hundredth—it had looked like Jessie, and yet, her face had been mangled, swollen, and bruised.

No. Tessa mentally shook her head. There was no way anyone could survive that. No way the CIA could be fooled into believing the dead woman was Jessica Mendoza.

And there was nothing she could do about it at the moment. She didn't have access to the video, which was on her laptop at her apartment. She couldn't reach out to anyone at Langley without raising questions. She couldn't ask Meg without revealing her suspicions, which could send Meg spiraling again.

Unless Meg was behind the cover-up.

Cover up? Tessa purposely pulled herself back from that ledge. She might not be the Agency's biggest fan, but not everything was a conspiracy. Tommy's spottings could simply be the result of an overwrought mind. Just like hers had been over her stepfather all these years.

Her brain circled back to Meg and the revelation about the virus.

If Meg had lied about it, she *could* be behind some bigger conspiracy that Flynn and the higher-ups had contrived—or quite possibly had no idea about. It might have nothing to do with Jessie's death, but it certainly had some connection.

Which would make Tessa's analysis of Meg all wrong.

When was the last time I was wrong about anyone?

Meg was an expert at a lot of things, and she knew how to contrive deep cover stories, but the shock, guilt, and grief she'd displayed after Jessie's death had been real. Tessa was sure of that.

Had someone tricked them all?

The window had fogged with her accelerated breathing. She swallowed and forced her pulse to slow. To steady her breath. *Stay in character.* She was nothing but a nondescript traveler on her way to the next stop.

Meanwhile, her brain continued to churn. If Tommy was correct, and Meg had lied about Del not triggering the virus on the USB... Then what?

Then Meg didn't trust Tessa.

Fair enough. Tessa had thrown everything back at her, refusing to officially join the team and making her stance on the Agency clear. Meg wasn't about to share classified information under the circumstances, and Tessa would have done the same in her shoes.

But suspecting there was something else going on behind the scenes made the whole thing not sit right with her.

Trust was a weapon. You could never have true friends when you were a spy. Conrad Flynn had taught them all that.

The train brakes hissed as it slowed to navigate a bend. Tessa briefly glanced toward Tommy, who was in an aisle seat facing her direction and drumming his fingers on the table between him and his fellow passengers. At least, he'd given up staring a hole in her. Only his profile was visible now, and although he appeared calm and detached as he read something on his burner phone, she detected the strain around his eyes and mouth.

A mouth she'd kissed and wanted to again.

Like her, his neutral expression was a shield. A calculated façade. She wanted to talk to him about Jessie, the virus, and everything—but maintaining their cover was critical. They had to appear as strangers. They'd fumbled at the station with their banter and his impulsive dash into the crowd, but no one had seemed to notice. Still, Tessa's training and instinct told her not to take chances. The shooter from the previous day materialized in her mind, and she gave the compartment a casual scan of those she could see. No one stood out to her, and none of the faces resembled Jessie at all.

Her mind replayed the chase—the shot that shattered the glass but would have missed entirely if she hadn't pivoted. The way the shooter had caught up to them in the alley but missed again when she'd fired and then abandoned the pursuit.

Amateur or professional? Could be either, depending on the outcome they'd been after.

Could it be the Jessie imposter?

Could it be Jessie?

Tessa shut down the impossible thought, even as those pesky doubts lingered and continued to gnaw at her. If Jessie was alive, what did that mean? Why would she keep it a secret? Why would she shoot at Tessa and Tommy?

Was she tied to the pending EMP attacks?

Tessa's pulse spiked again, her breath catching at the idea of such a betrayal. It was too much, even for her jaded heart and cynical mind. Until she could get some solid answers to her questions, all she was doing was creating more dragons to slay.

Her phone vibrated, the sound muffled in her pocket but still jarring. She had two now, and this wasn't the burner that only Tommy had the number to. She frowned, angling the screen so her neighbor couldn't read it.

Spence.

In all the time she'd known him, he'd only ever contacted her directly a few times. They'd always been friends but not teammates. Why was he calling now? To join Meg's recruitment campaign?

"Hey," she answered stiffly. "What's going on?"

"Oh, you know: Meg and Dec fighting. Flynn yelling. End of the world shit." He gave a half-hearted chuckle. "I should ask you the same thing. What's going on?"

She glanced at the passengers in her booth. "I'm heading to London for a few days. I'm on the train now. I'll call you back once I've landed, okay?"

"Don't lie to me."

She should hang up. Pretend she'd settled things with her caller, and all was fine. "I know why you're calling, and I'm sorry, but the answer is no. I can't. Talk soon!"

"Tess, wait, *luv*." His voice softened, catching her before she could disconnect. "I know I don't say this often, but I care about you. We all do."

His admission took her by surprise. Something inside her that was hard and cold melted a little. Out of all of them, he could do that to her—make her feel more human.

"Look, *luv*," she warned, using his term because she didn't want to say his name. It was an old habit, born of her training, but using real names, even over a secure line, was dangerous.

He bulldozed over her. "I cared about Jessie, too." His

voice cracked, and its roughness surprised her as much as his previous admission. "More than just a teammate. I never told her. Never told anyone. I don't wanna make that mistake again. I want you to know that, regardless of whether you join the team or not, I have the utmost admiration and respect for you. You've been a true friend, and I appreciate that. They're hard to come by in our line of work."

Tessa's pulse skipped and then hammered hard. It was as if he had read her thoughts. She pressed her back into the seat, wishing she could disappear into it. "She knew."

The return shocked silence told her she'd surprised *him* this time. "She did?" His voice hitched. "You're saying Jessie knew I..."

"That you were in love with her, yes." In some way, they all had been. Jessie had been a free spirit while being so good at her job. She'd made everyone believe they were special. Made them all think that she would do anything for them, no matter the consequences. No matter what the mission took out of her or what line she might have to cross to protect them.

She had given each of them the rarest gift of friendship—total and unconditional loyalty.

She was one of the few I trusted.

The realization caught her in the chest, and she hiccupped. One of the men across from her glanced up at the sound, and she quickly focused on the landscape flying by the window again.

"Did she feel the same about me?" Spence's vulnerability was evident in his words.

This was the last place she wanted to have this conversation, but she felt she owed him that much. "I don't know. I wish I could say yes, but I think she was afraid to let herself form a relationship with someone like you."

"Someone like me?" His tone was offended. "What's that supposed to mean? "

The man across from her returned to his laptop. "Not what you think. You were a teammate. She had deep feelings for you, that I do know, but romantic ones? I'm sorry. I can't verify that."

"Ever the analyst," he chuckled. "At least she didn't die not knowing how I felt. I guess that's something, eh?"

"It is." She could give him that much. "Say, I have a question for you."

He gave a resigned sigh at the change of subject. "Shoot."

Although the others seemed busy, she feared she'd garnered their interest. "Hold on, will you?" She rose and made for the aisle.

Tommy looked up, his Tessa radar instantly on alert and burning a hole into her back as she headed for the restroom. She didn't speak again until she was locked inside. "You're my favorite tech guy, and I have a question. If Tommy planted a virus on the USB Meg and Dec recovered from the embassy, would Del miss it?"

He hesitated. "What are you asking?"

"If you think it's possible he missed such a glaring thing."

"Of course, it's possible. Del's good—the best we've got—but even the best make mistakes. You know that."

It wasn't meant to pierce her heart, but it did. She'd been the best at what she did once. And yes, she'd made mistakes.

She wondered now if one of them had been recommending Jessie for the Black Swan Division. Meg, Dec, and Spence had no idea that Flynn had put Tessa on the spot about it when he'd come to her, telling her about Meg's brilliant idea. One he wished he had come up with himself.

"There's something else," Spence said. "Before the drive was wiped, Del found something that changes the game."

The train swayed, and she gripped the sink card to keep her balance. Spence had to know that Meg hadn't told her, and if he was volunteering it, he was going against the unspoken rule of the team—only Meg got to share classified information. That fact had to be bugging Spence enough to break protocol and share it with her. She didn't question why. "You're treading on dangerous ground if you tell me."

"I've never backed away from dangerous plays before. And just like confessing about my love for Jessie and how important you are to me, I need to do this."

This could be treason. Treason against the swans, against the CIA itself. If they found out, he'd need a good lawyer. "You better be sure. I'm not officially one of your team."

"I don't know what game you're running, Tessa, but you *are* one of us. You can deny it all day long, but I don't buy it. I'm telling you because you need to know in order to watch your back. If I didn't say something and you were hurt or killed..." He cleared his throat. "If you tell anyone I am your source, I'll deny it."

It wasn't a threat—he was simply letting her know she didn't need to worry about him. "You better. I'm listening."

"There is evidence suggesting that someone quite familiar with how the Agency works is framing us for the coming EMP attacks."

The train jolted as it hit a rough patch of track, pitching her sideways. Her knees buckled, and only her grip on the sink kept her upright. "*What?*"

"They're manipulating global events to destabilize power structures and pin the blame on us."

Her blood ran cold. "Someone inside the CIA?"

"Either that or a former operative. It has to be someone with a lot of connections and resources. They've got access to intel that only certain people should. Could be someone high up in the ranks or someone who was at one time."

"Or someone very familiar with the swans."

He caught her gist. "Tommy?"

She shook her head, catching sight of her pale face in the mirror over the sink. The announcement for their next stop crackled over the speakers. "I have to go," she said. "Thanks for the heads up. If this is true, you need to watch *your* back. Don't worry about mine."

She cut off the call before Spencer could reply and shoved the phone into her pocket. As she left the restroom and returned to her seat, she avoided Tommy's inquisitive gaze.

A former CIA employee framing the swans for the attacks? Tommy had only been an analyst. Or had he? She'd already found herself questioning that. Her skin crawled as she sank into her seat.

Had he been lying all this time?

Feeling his gaze still on her, she raised her own to meet his down the aisle. If he'd lied to her, if he was using her...

She gripped the armrest, realizing the predicament she was now in. Helping a traitor. Hell, he might be pinning the whole thing on her.

As the train began to slow, carrying them to their next destination, her gut cramped. *Stupid.* She'd been so damn stupid.

And now, she would have to become the ultimate spy so she could turn the tables on him.

TWELVE

Tommy gripped the leather strap of his carry-on as he stepped through the Arrivals Gate at Heathrow. He scanned the area, then marched across the pale marble floor crisscrossed with darker veins, searching for Tessa.

The steady hum of announcements filtered through his thoughts, but his attention was honed in on the people milling about. Faces blurred together, none of them familiar. He hated this. Being alone in a crowd was nothing new to him, but the separation from Tessa was like being underwater and needing oxygen.

She'd booked separate flights. He should have expected it, considering she wanted them to travel as strangers, but it had still caught him off guard. At least he'd made it through with no issues, his new passport solid.

Once they'd arrived at Sibiu, she'd refused to explain the details of her mysterious call. Something was up, though, and he was mad as hell at her resolute, unwavering insistence on keeping it a secret. He tried texting her on their burner phones several times. He called her once. She ignored him.

Now, here he was, scanning the inside of the airport like a lost puppy while she was who knew where.

His connecting flight didn't leave for two hours. Two hours, and he would be on his way back to America. He wondered if she would be there when he arrived. Maybe she'd gotten cold feet after that phone call. For all he knew, she wasn't even in London.

A man approached, holding a placard with a single name scrawled in neat letters. *Mathers*. At first, Tommy forgot his alias, but then he realized the guy was beelining for him. He tensed. "You looking for me?"

"Yes, sir," the man said. His crisp accent was smooth, polished British, and it reminded Tommy of his days at The Farm, where his training had taught him how to pick apart authenticity. This guy was the real deal. "The Architect sent me."

Tessa. Relief relaxed his shoulders. Maybe they would finally meet up again. After following the man through the crowded airport, he stepped outside into a foggy, rainy mist. He climbed into the sleek, black car waiting at the curb, the leather interior smelling faintly of bergamot.

They drove out of the city and onto winding country roads. Tommy pulled out his phone to text Tessa, feeling uneasy about it, but found she had already messaged him. *I'm waiting.*

A castle appeared on the horizon, modest by royal

standards but still carrying the kind of old money charm that screamed exclusivity. Looming in muted gray stone, with ivy creeping up its sides and luxuriant gardens, it seemed to belong more to the landscape than the people who lived there.

Who *did* live there?

Tommy whistled under his breath. "What is this place? "

The man seemed confused by the question. "The Grand Fox. It belongs to Ms. Vulpe."

Tessa, always surprising him. She'd claimed her mother had given up her rights to her family's royal holdings, but this? This was out of a storybook, and if it belonged to Tessa, it meant there was more to that story.

Or that she'd lied.

He shook his head, hoping it wasn't the latter.

The drive was a substantial U-shaped stone path, a three-tiered fountain in its center. The butler opened the double entry doors who seemed straight out of central casting, his black tails immaculate, and his hair slicked back without a single strand out of place. "Mr. Mathers, welcome," he said, motioning for Tommy to enter. "I'm Clarence."

The interior was...a lot. Thick Persian rugs blanketed the floors, muffling his footsteps as he followed the butler down the hall. Chandeliers hung from overhead, casting light that glinted off polished wood and the gilded picture frames lining the walls. Those frames held portraits of severe men and women who stared down at him, their eyes dripping judgment. Even the air smelled expensive—like old books and lemon furniture polish.

Tommy couldn't decide if he wanted to laugh at the pretension or run.

On one hand, he didn't blame Tessa's mother for giving this up. On the other, he had to question her sanity.

"Ms. Vulpe is expecting you," Clarence said, stopping at a set of tall, double doors.

When they opened, a maid was there who led him deeper into the mansion and into a room that felt stuffier than the rest of the house, which was saying something. It was all dark paneling, heavy drapes, and velvet furniture. A Victorian drama theater stage that had been left to collect dust.

But there she was.

Tessa stood by the window, her silhouette lit by the fading afternoon light. When she faced him, the usual spark in her gaze was tempered. "Thank you," she said to the maid, her voice carrying a clipped authority. The woman dipped her chin and disappeared, leaving them alone as she closed the doors behind her.

"Nice digs," Tommy said. His bag thumped to the floor as he released it. "Didn't peg you for the aristocrat type, especially after what you told me about your mom leaving all this behind."

"I was told she had, but a few years ago, an attorney for the estate reached out to me. This place belonged to my grandparents. They've passed on, and with my mother gone as well, the place became mine. I plan to sell it, but I haven't gotten around to it yet." Her fingers traveled over the edges of the furniture and fireplace. "It's useful when I need somewhere no one would think to look for me. Also"—her gaze pinned him again—"when I need to interrogate someone."

He stiffened. "Are you going to explain what that means, or should I start guessing?"

She gracefully lifted a snifter of dark liquid as she scanned him from head to toe. He felt like he was under a microscope. "I know about your plan. How you've set me up. Set up the swans."

The air left his lungs. "What are you talking about?"

She used the glass to point at a chair. "Destabilizing global power structures and framing them for it. All the while, you've acted as if you're on the trail of the Russian investors and their conspirators. You convinced me that you want to stop the EMP attacks when, in reality, you're working with the Russians to execute them."

He blinked. "Are you drunk?"

"Don't tell me you're not involved." She swished the liquor around in the glass. "It's clever, I'll give you that. And Jessie? Making us all believe she's dead while she's orchestrating it behind the scenes. Wow. You really had me going on that one. Meg, too."

"Wait, *what*? Making you believe she's dead? She *is* dead, Tessa. And I'm not working with the Russians. For God's sake, where the hell is this coming from? Meg?"

Her laugh was bitter. "Whose idea was it? Yours or Jessie's?"

"Have you lost your freaking mind?"

"I can't believe I fell for it. For..." She gestured at him. "You and your act."

"I'm *not* acting." He crossed the room to stand in front of her. "What happened on the train? Who called you?"

"Spence. He told me all about a mole framing the swans for the attacks. I knew you wanted revenge for Jessie's death, and I might have understood your actions if that were the only part of it, but the two of you betrayed all of us? How could you?"

"I have no idea what you're talking about. Yeah, I wanted vengeance on Mosai Hagar, and yes, I want those Russian bastards to pay for what they're about to do, but... You think I'm working with them? That Jessie's alive and we're conspiring against the CIA? Seriously, what have you been smoking, woman?"

"Just tell me the truth."

"I am telling the truth!" Disbelief tightened his throat. "I would never betray you, and yes, I have issues with the swans, but... How can you think I'd do such a thing? Not just to them, but with the EMP attacks to the soldiers at the bases? To the innocent people who'd be affected by them? Jesus." He jammed his hand through his hair and paced away from her. He turned back. "You know me better than that, Tessa."

"Do I?" For a long moment, she studied him with that unreadable expression of hers.

He let her see it on his face. No subterfuge. No lies.

Seeming to come to some decision, she blew out a

long sigh. "This is why I can't be a spy. I can't constantly wonder if someone is betraying me."

"I'm not."

Another long look. "I analyze people to figure out their intentions, but I also have an internal radar that never steers me wrong. You've upset that radar. It feels... off."

What was he supposed to say? "Sorry...?"

"I don't want to have feelings for you. That's the problem."

Again, was he supposed to apologize? Screw that. "I'm not a traitor. I'm not working with one. I swear to you, I will never hurt you or betray your trust."

For the third time, all she did was size him up. As if it took everything she had, she finally gave a nod and motioned him to follow her. "I want to show you something."

He joined her at the desk, where a laptop was open. She hit a couple of keys, and the screen displayed a grainy video feed. He squinted at it, recognizing the setting. "The train station?"

"You, Spence, and Del are gifted at this technology, but I'm not without resources. This is from the station's CCTV. Watch."

She clicked the play button, and he leaned closer. On screen, people moved along one of the hallways. He scanned them before she stopped the feed, rewound it, and played it again. "What am I looking for?"

"I think you know." She rewound the feed a second time and hit play.

His stomach bottomed out. What she'd said about Jessie...

Sure enough, this time, when he scanned the crowd, he saw a hooded figure that made his breath catch. The woman did her best to stay behind a group of taller individuals, but several times, as she made her way down the hall, at least part of her face was visible.

"It can't be," he whispered.

"I can't confirm it's her without running this through facial recognition," Tessa said. Her voice sounded distant, overly detached. "But if this *is* Jessie, she's been alive this whole time."

His mind raced, memories of his sister's death replaying like a broken film reel. Mosai Hagar. The swing of the machete. The blood.

But he'd found circumstantial evidence that suggested Jessie might've been tied to Hager and the Russian investors. Evidence he couldn't allow himself to believe.

And hadn't shared with anyone. Not even Tessa.

He closed his eyes and bowed his head. "There's no way. We saw her die." His voice broke on the last word.

"We saw *someone* die," Tessa corrected. He heard the snap of the laptop closing. "It smells like an elaborate cover-up."

He couldn't stay still, opening his eyes and turning away from her. Jessie was alive. She'd faked her death. Why? "I *have* been seeing her."

"Looks that way." She leaned a hip on the desk, her face still remote. "You said she knew about the superconductors and went to MediSune to speak to the developer. Maybe it wasn't because she was trying to stop the EMP attacks but because she was a co-conspirator in them. The question is, if she's betrayed her country and has been working with Hagar and the Russians, why has she been following you? My best guess is that she fears you're about to reveal her deception and expose the truth. I think she shot at us to scare us off."

He rubbed his hands over his face, trying to piece together a puzzle that refused to make sense. Tessa watched him as if she still wasn't sure she trusted him. It made him feel like an alien in his own skin.

"She's working with the Russians," Tessa said, as if driving the point home to keep him from further argument with himself. "That's the only explanation."

"No." His denial was automatic. He shook his head adamantly, even though he'd been worried about this exact thing. "She's no traitor. There has to be another explanation."

But even as the words hung in the air, doubt crept in, cold and unwelcome.

Tessa blew out a long, slow breath, her detachment melting away. A bleak sadness filled her eyes. "I want to believe that, too."

Hands on hips, he continued to pace the elegant room, feeling completely out of place. "The first thing we have to do is confirm it's her."

"Any idea how?"

He went to the desk, gesturing for her to move so he

could sit at the laptop. "She was hunting that Viktor fellow. Hagar was a lead, just like MediSune."

She shifted to stare over his shoulder as he began logging into his personal, encrypted files in the cloud. "If she wasn't a traitor, do you think Hagar knew she was on his trail?"

Flipping between theories—was Jessie a traitor working with Hagar and the Russians, or was she trying to expose them—made his head spin. "Yes, and if he was part of the larger coup to set up the swans for the attacks, that's why he singled her and Meg out that night. He wanted to expose the swans to the world."

When she saw him open a software program and drop a snapshot of Jessie's face from the station into it, she made a sound of appreciation. "You have your own version of facial recognition?"

"I borrowed some of the basic programming from our friends at the Agency, tweaked it, and created a bare bones version that I can run without them, or any other law enforcement service, knowing."

"I'm impressed."

He glanced over his shoulder. "I still can't believe you thought I was behind all this."

"I'm jaded. You know that."

Not an apology. His chest, already caving in, tweaked. She was right—he did know it. He shouldn't be surprised.

"Why has she been following you?" Tessa paced the rug. "She's too sloppy to let herself be seen, and yet, you detected her three times. And how did she follow us to the train station?"

He didn't have answers to those questions. Again, her analysis was correct—if Jessie didn't want to be seen, she wouldn't be. It was sloppy for her to have gotten close enough that he could make her out in a crowd. Had she been counting on him not to believe his own eyes?

"If she *is* alive...." His voice choked again, the ramifications ramming into him like a tidal wave. "I just can't..."

"I know." She placed a hand on his shoulder. It was warm and heavy, reassuring. "We'll figure it out."

He glanced at the clock in the upper right-hand corner of the screen. "Our plane..."

"The plan has changed. We won't be going to Arizona. Not yet, anyway." She grabbed her cell phone off the desk. "I'm going to make a few calls. You're going to check your clothes and bag to make sure there's no tracking device hidden in them."

Before either of them could say another word, the software program pinged.

There, on the screen, the shot from the train station up on the left, and a clearer photo taken from a CIA personnel file came on the right. Red dots highlighted the matching features in each image—there were only three, and only on the right side of her face.

But it was enough.

Tessa clenched her phone as Tommy swore under his breath.

Confirmation.

Jessie Mendoza was alive.

THIRTEEN

Tessa gripped Tommy's shoulder again. He vibrated under her hand with a coiling intensity that she felt in her chest as well.

Evening had crept into the room from the narrow windows that faced the east gardens. The landscaping of well-manicured hedges and walking paths was already settling under a blanket of shadows.

Her heart ached. Her body did, too. She was exhausted by this cat-and-mouse game.

Maybe she was a fool, but she wanted to comfort Tommy. To believe he was innocent. That he hadn't tricked her. Betrayed her.

Not like Jessie had.

If he had, she might break and never be able to put herself together again.

Jessie's deception and treachery shredded her in a way she hadn't felt since the night she'd witnessed her mother's murder. How could she have been so stupid as to let herself get close to someone again? To allow her emotions to override her logic?

The voice inside her head demanded she cut herself some slack. The deception was first rate. She wasn't even sure that Hagar had realized he hadn't killed Jessie. Whoever the stand-in had been, they'd played the part perfectly. Had the woman even known what was going to happen to her?

Tessa gripped her cramping stomach. She couldn't wrap her mind around the fact that Jessie would allow such a thing, but then none of this aligned with the person she'd known. That they'd all known.

Or thought they had.

"Why didn't you become an operative?" she asked Tommy. It was time to put a few of her doubts to rest. "You have the skills. It comes naturally to you."

His body slumped, a bone-weary exhaustion coloring his voice. "Just because I'm good at it doesn't mean I like it. I saw what the missions did to Jessie. What her life did to the two of us." He tapped the keyboard, his fingers flying so fast that she couldn't read the code he was entering. "She was gone for months at a time without any communication. I had no idea where she was, what was going on, or if she was in danger. I hated it. At least as an analyst, I could discreetly check up on the swans. I had to be careful and not trip any flags Del put on their files, but I could occasionally find out where she was and what she was working on."

"It must've been hard."

He paused, typing to glance at her, hearing the sincerity in her voice. "Tough for you, too, wasn't it? You were close with her and Meg. You never knew if they would make it back from their missions."

She turned her back on him, staring out the window as the gardens grew darker and the solar lights flared to life. "Flynn originally recruited me for the swans, and I told him Jessie was a better candidate. I was right, of course, but after her death"—she hesitated—"her *pseudo* death, I guess, I blamed myself for it. It should've been me that died that day, not her."

He abandoned the desk and came to her, standing behind her close enough that she could feel his body heat. "You've blamed yourself all this time?"

A bitter laugh slid from between her lips. "Seems all of us have been caring around guilt over her death. It appears to be wasted emotion."

Like all the emotions she'd felt for people over the years.

His hand touched her lower back. "I'm sorry."

She swiveled enough to stare up into his handsome face. The distress she saw there made her heart clench. The deeply creased brow, the tightness around his lips and eyes, the anger simmering underneath his still-obvious shock—she felt it all, too. "You have nothing to be sorry for. You're a victim in all this, just like the rest of us."

"I still can't believe she would intentionally betray us and her country." He dropped his hand and rubbed his eyes. "Until I prove she's guilty, I'm giving her the benefit of the doubt. There's too much about this that we don't know."

She cupped his cheek, his short beard tickling her palm. He still had hope. Hadn't had such things stomped out of him. "I wish I'd had a brother like you growing up."

He slid his fingers around her wrist, drawing her hand to his lips. They grazed her palm, and his eyes turned darker. "You have me now," he said so softly that it sent a shiver of desire through her.

His breath was warm against her skin, and that tight control she kept on things splintered. She hadn't allowed herself to feel anything for anyone since Jessie's death, and that death had been thrown in her face like ice water.

But Tommy had shown up on her doorstep, wounded in more ways than one. Despite Meg's recruitment efforts, Tessa might have joined the swans just to find him. She hadn't needed to, though. He'd come to her. Not Meg or anyone else. Tommy trusted *her*. He *still* trusted her, and she could see his heart in his eyes, so soulful, so devastated.

She slid her hand to his neck, parting her lips and easing closer to him in an open invitation.

He grabbed her by the waist and pulled her close, dropping his mouth to hers.

Tessa's world dissolved. Surprise mingled with relief as she realized how desperately she'd needed this release from the suffocating fear that had gripped her since the revelation about Jessie being alive.

As their tongues danced, their bodies pressed closer,

and for a fleeting moment, she could pretend that the shadows weren't closing in, that she was just a woman in the arms of the man she loved.

Love. It couldn't be. She would *never* let herself be so vulnerable.

His strong hands molded her against him, solid and unyielding, as if he could ward off the demons nipping at her heels. In this stolen moment, she wanted to believe in loyalty and courage and trust someone else with her heart. After all, hadn't he risked everything to protect her? Hadn't he proven himself worthy of her faith?

Tessa's resistance crumbled like sand under his passionate onslaught, and with a shaky sigh, she allowed her defenses to drop. Tommy's groan of triumph spurred her on, their kisses deepening and intensifying with each passing second. His hands slid up her back, and then he deftly freed her from her clothes.

First, her shirt.

Next, her bra.

He stepped back. Cool air caressed her heated skin, and she ached for more as he openly raked his gaze over her shoulders and breasts.

With a growl, he scooped her into his arms and carried her to the nearest sofa. His hungry eyes held hers as he lowered her onto the cushions.

She slipped out of her slacks as he discarded his clothes carelessly on the floor. His body was a work of art, honed and taut, and she couldn't take her eyes off him.

Tommy joined her on the sofa, his muscles flexing as

he circled one of her nipples with his thumb, gazing into her eyes. "Are you sure about this?"

She nodded, her heart in her throat. "I'm sure."

A soft smile curved his lips as he brushed a stray hair from her face. "God, I've wanted you for so long," he whispered before his lips found hers again.

His hands roamed her body, memorizing every curve and secret place. With each touch, she felt herself opening up to him in ways she'd never thought possible. He made her feel safe and cherished, and she was utterly consumed by desire for him.

She trembled under the touch of his hands, her body a canvas for his exploration. He touched and kissed and licked every inch, building the throb between her legs until she thought she'd go mad.

Tommy's muscles rippled beneath her hands as he moved on top of her. She tasted the salt of his skin as she kissed his throat, his chest. Her tongue left a trail of wet heat, and she wanted to switch positions so she could get access to parts lower.

Tommy had other ideas.

A symphony of moans and gasps escaped her lips when he sucked at her neck, then lowered his mouth to each of her breasts. Her breathing was already ragged and desperate. His fingertips traced patterns on her skin as he went lower and lower, leaving a trail of fire in their wake. She closed her eyes, arching into his mouth as he lowered it to the aching spot between her legs.

His hands were rough yet gentle as they pushed her

knees wider to give him full access. She surrendered to his exploration with a mixture of vulnerability and desire. He slipped his tongue inside, a skilled artist tracing every contour with tenderness and reverence. Stroke after stroke, she felt as though a new chapter was being written in the story of her body.

As her climax hit, Tessa stuffed her doubts and fears to the back of her mind, allowing herself to drown in the sensations he evoked in her. "Tommy," she cried out.

He kept up his onslaught until the orgasm subsided, then let her surf the bliss as he teased his fingers over her hips, across her stomach, and laid a hand on her chest. She cracked open her eyes to see him staring at her. "I love to feel your heartbeat," he said, pressing his palm more firmly to her chest where her heart was thudding wildly.

Staring into his face, she felt the walls she'd erected around her heart replaced by a blissful abandon she'd never thought possible. "We're not done," she murmured.

His grin was pure alpha male.

He produced a condom from his discarded pants. "Found them at your place. I don't want to think about who's been in your bed, but I'm glad for the stash."

"I never felt anything for them," she admitted. *Not like I do you.*

He returned, the heat in his gaze as he surveyed her from the tips of her toes to her mouth, smoldering. Her knees, still open and exposing her most vulnerable area, started to close, but he pinned them down, kissed her deeply, and entered her in one swift stroke.

Her swollen folds resisted, and she cried into his mouth. His lips and tongue teased her as he settled and held still, giving her a moment to adjust to his size.

Her muscles unclenched, and desire spread through her again. She adjusted her hips, taking him even deeper.

"God, Tessa," he moaned, scoring her neck with his teeth.

She shivered. "Make it good," she ordered.

He chuckled. "I might need to practice a lot in order to perfect my skills."

"We'll see."

She expected hard, fast thrusts, but he kept her pinned in place as he took his time with her. Their bodies moved together in a sensual rhythm, skin glistening in the dim light of the room. His eyes locked on hers, conveying a raw desire and understanding that made her feel vulnerable in other ways.

As they built to a fresh climax, her skin grew hot and slick again. Every touch ignited sparks of pleasure coiling at the base of her spine. She cried out as the release barreled through her, clasping his broad shoulders as she spun out into nothingness.

Two more strokes, her nails scoring his back, and he followed her over into the abyss.

When they came up from those depths, gasping and spent, he wrapped her in his arms, their bodies entwined. Their breathing ragged, they stared into each other's eyes, both acutely aware that nothing would ever be the same between them again.

But as Tessa drifted off to sleep in Tommy's arms, the

ghosts of their pasts lingered in the shadows, their malev-olent presence a constant reminder that their respite was only temporary. The game they were playing was far from over, and the stakes had just become immeasurably higher.

FOURTEEN

The first thing Tommy noticed when he woke in the all-white bedroom wasn't the room, but the warmth pressed against his side.

Tessa.

Her head rested on his shoulder, her breath soft and steady against his chest. For a moment, the mission that had felt like a horror show felt distant, almost like it belonged to someone else.

He tightened his arm around her instinctively, his hand brushing the underside of her breast. He trailed his lips over her shoulder. She'd left the bandage off her wound, and he could see it was healing.

Last night, they'd both needed an anchor, a tether to steady them after the realization that Jessie wasn't dead. Worse, she might be an active participant in something treasonous.

He refused to believe that his sister was anything but the morally upstanding person he'd relied on his whole life. There had to be more to it, and he knew it was going to be ugly, but he held onto that anchor even more now. The anchor that gave him hope that she had a good reason for what she'd done.

He couldn't imagine what that would be. Couldn't accept that she'd been alive all this time and misled them into believing she was dead. He wasn't sure there was anything that could excuse that.

Tessa stirred, burrowing closer as if reluctant to wake and face the day. He brushed his mouth over her temple. "You're hogging the covers," he murmured. The blanket was squarely over both of them, but teasing her awake came naturally.

Her lashes fluttered open. She squinted at him, her voice groggy but sarcastic. "That's because you failed to keep me warm in this drafty old place."

Sarcasm was good. "Is that so?" He kissed her cheek, jawline, and ear, earning an annoyed huff from her. He pulled back the blanket and began trailing light fingertips over her bare chest, stomach, and hip. Her annoyance turned to squirming, and she slapped at his hand, laughing and pulling away.

He grabbed her and drew her under him, kissing her thoroughly. Of course, that led to more things, and soon they were entangled in each other and the sheets, finding a quick morning release.

Still breathing hard, she jumped when a knock sounded at the bedroom door.

"Breakfast is served in the dining room," came the maid's voice. Tommy had learned her name was Moda.

His driver at the airport was Randall. "Or would you prefer it in here, m'Lady?"

Tommy nibbled at her ear as she replied, giving a little squeal. "Dining room. We'll be there shortly."

"As you wish." Moda's footsteps faded away.

Tommy rolled onto his side, propping himself up on one elbow as he grinned down at her. "We didn't order breakfast."

"It comes with the place." She pushed at his shoulder and swung her legs over the side of the bed. "Come on. We've got Russians to catch and ghosts to chase."

His grin faltered. "Right. Russians, and ghosts. Can't wait."

They cleaned up quickly, and he held her hand as they wandered through hallways and landings until they found the dining room.

Breakfast was worthy of the estate, from poached eggs to freshly baked pastries that Tommy couldn't resist. "So, this is how the other half lives," he said around a bite of quiche and a swig of freshly squeezed orange juice.

Tessa gave him a wry look over her cup of tea. "Finish your proper English breakfast. We have a lot to do."

As soon as the plates were cleared, they went to an office. It didn't look like her—more like a stuffy older man's den--one who had too much money.

But money provided high-end technology. Tommy commandeered her laptop from the desk, his fingers flying over the keys as he dug into surveillance footage, cross-referencing it with timestamps from his previous sightings of Jessie.

He'd never thought to look before, but one of the videos he found from a security camera across the street from the cemetery showed a woman who could pass for Jessie. She was dressed in black and wearing a large, flamboyant hat and sunglasses.

While he continued digging for footage from cameras around the embassy, Tessa made phone calls. Hearing only her side of them didn't always make sense, but he lost himself in the following video clip from near the US Embassy in Bucharest—his last station. His gut twisted as he watched what appeared to be his sister approaching an older man in an impeccable suit a block from the embassy's parking lot the day he'd spotted her. Their exchange was brief—a handshake, a few words—and then she'd climbed into a black Land Rover, and they'd driven off.

Tommy froze the frame on the license plate. "Got you," he whispered. He zoomed in on it—diplomatic plates.

It didn't take long for him to trace the vehicle. It was registered to the LLC shell company he'd been investigating before the embassy riots—Kaltrain. A quick review of company records showed ties to a network of other LLCs and businesses he'd already connected to the Russian investors. The diplomatic tie was nonexistent, a cover.

Searching public databases, he combed through layers of bullshit records to find what he needed. He leaned back in the chair, catching Tessa while she was on hold. "I've got an address for this LLC."

"Ilford?" she asked.

He nodded, feeling the rush of adrenaline. Finally, they were on to something.

Tessa paced, the phone pressed to her ear as she worked an angle. She held up a finger to him as her call went through. Posing as a CIA employee, she introduced herself, putting the call on speaker for him to hear. "Dr. DeAnna Wyn." She was using her professional librarian voice. "I'm Contessa Vulpe from the Counterterrorism Department at the CIA. I'm following up on your meeting with Jessica Mendoza last year. Could you tell me about that discussion involving the superconductors she inquired about?"

The woman on the other end took a moment before responding. "I'm sorry. Who did you say you are?"

Tessa repeated her fake credentials. They'd been real at one time. "I'm following up on Ms. Mendoza's files. Can you confirm the manufacturer of the superconductors?"

"I don't remember."

"You met with her on July seventeenth, correct? She had concerns about the ones your company placed in a set of military computers. Those are top-secret, special orders. You don't remember?"

The accusation riled the doctor, and her reply was gruff. "I can confirm that I spoke to her. She wanted to know the process for the orders and how many had been shipped to the Department of Defense. She had clearance papers, so I shared that information. Until you have the same papers, this conversation is over."

"I can put you through to my boss right now if you'd prefer to speak to him. He's the grumpy, stressed-out director of Intelligence. Not a pleasant fellow, but it's up to you."

Dr. Wyn seemed to weigh her options. "I'd have to look up the details."

"Did Ms. Mendoza ask about a man named Viktor?"

A pregnant pause filled the air. "Why don't you ask her yourself?"

"Because she's dead."

There was a gasp, followed by a rushed response: "I'm sorry," the doctor said. "I can't help you."

The line went dead.

Tessa cursed under her breath, slapping the desktop with her palm. "I can't tell if she was unnerved about the name or about Jessie being dead. She must not have seen the video or realized from the social media outcry after-ward that she'd spoken to the victim of it." Tessa tapped her phone against her chin. "I sure would like to get a bug on her phone. We might have to go to Arizona after all."

"Not necessary." Tommy clicked the mouse several times and entered the woman's phone number into one of his software programs. "I learned this from a Chinese hacker. All I have to do is sync the software with her number..."

The laptop speaker suddenly picked up the sound of a ringing phone. Tommy grinned at Tessa. "Looks like our doctor is making a call."

They could only hear her end of the conversation, and Tommy made sure to record it so they could replay it once they were done. Whoever picked up listened as the doctor gave them a replay of her conversation with Tessa. The person asked several questions, none of which the doctor could answer, about Tessa's true identity or why she would be asking about the superconductors or Viktor's name. It was obvious by her tone, which became more high-pitched and panicky, that whoever she spoke with had concerns that made the doctor even more uncomfortable.

The call didn't last long, but it was enough for him to get the recipient's number. After it ended, he fed that number into another piece of the software program with a database the CIA would be envious of. He watched as it filtered through millions of phones until it found a match. His screen lit up, a soft confirmative beep emitting from the speaker.

"Kaltrain," he muttered. Satisfaction made his grin turn predatory as he met Tessa's eyes. "The same LLC as the Land Rover."

She moved to peer over his shoulder. Her breath tickled his ear. "Can you cross-reference it along with that number to the name Viktor?"

"On it."

He fed the information into a public search engine. Sometimes, the simplest way was also the quickest. A dozen hits came up, three of them with the name Viktor Renard.

"Renard," Tommy read aloud. He switched screens, scanning a website for one of the dozen LLCs he'd been investigating. "Why does that sound familiar? Ah... there you are." He tapped the screen as a photo appeared from a publicity shot at a board meeting. "V.C. Renard. He's one of the board members but listed as absentee the night this photo was taken. His picture doesn't appear in any of this company's PR or social media, even though his name is on all the documentation and paperwork."

When Tessa didn't say anything, he twisted to look at her. Her face had gone slack, pale. "What is it?"

She swallowed. "Renard means fox in French. My last name—Vulpe—means fox in Latin."

"That's a weird coincidence."

"There are no coincidences in this line of work."

"You think there's a link between you and this Viktor guy?"

The laptop chimed with a traffic alert. He opened the notification box. "The Rover just pinged a traffic cam." A side-by-side map showed the location. "It's here. In London."

When he met her eyes, he saw she didn't believe this was a coincidence, either. "Not Ilford?" she asked.

He shook his head. "It's near Heathrow."

The airport.

That rush of adrenaline spiked. Had someone—Jessie?—followed them here?

"We might be able to catch it," she said, detached again and seeming to read his mind.

He closed the laptop, swiped it off the desk, and stood. "Let's go."

FIFTEEN

The Mercedes SUV hummed outside the castle's grand entrance, its polished frame gleaming in the midday sun. Tessa would never get used to such extravagance, but it did come in handy right now.

Clarence held open the rear passenger door, his crisp uniform immaculate as always.

"I should drive," Tommy said, flicking his gaze from the butler to her. "We can't afford to lose whoever's in the Land Rover."

Tessa slipped into the backseat. "You don't know the streets like Clarence does. Get in."

Tommy stood immobile and unconvinced. Clarence gave him a patient smile—one he'd used on Tessa since her inaugural visit after discovering her grandparents had left the estate to her. "Sir, I assure you, I'm more than capable. I've been trained in both offensive and defensive driving. You're in good hands."

"No offense," Tommy said, "but this may turn into more than a simple trip to the airport."

Her emotions tumbled around inside her. Impatience took the reins. "Fine. Leave him, Clarence."

"As you wish, my Lady."

Surprise, surprise, Tommy slid in beside her. "Nice try."

Clarence caught her eye and winked before shutting the door and hurrying to his seat. They wheeled out of the circular drive and were off, the sharp acceleration pressing her and Tommy into the leather cushions.

"Better put on your seatbelt," Tessa advised Tommy.

When they bounced onto the road, he did.

As the castle disappeared behind them, Tommy opened the laptop and checked the map. "It's still there. Must be waiting for someone."

Tessa watched the countryside blur past, her mind conjuring too many foreboding ideas. Viktor Renard. Kaltrain.

Her stepfather's voice echoed in her mind, uninvited. "*My little fox,*" he'd called her. When her mother had married him, she'd replaced Vulpe with his last name at his request. And yet, Harris Brewer had taught Tessa the word 'fox' in a dozen languages: French, Russian, Romanian. The last of which was identical to the Latin form. It had been a game, the way he'd used the various versions as nicknames for her. Only when she'd gotten older and was living with her aunt had she realized he'd used it as a way of taunting her mother—reminding her that Tessa wasn't his child.

When she'd turned eighteen, Tessa had returned her surname to Vulpe.

"Hey," Tommy said, sliding a finger down her arm. "You okay?"

"Just thinking." She couldn't admit the truth—she was freaking the hell out. Thinking sounded better. Professional. In control.

All of which she wasn't.

"Thinking about this Viktor fellow?"

She opened a search engine on her phone, her fingers hovering over the keyboard. "And other things." It was a stupid idea, but she had to know. She typed in Harris J. Brewer, her stepfather's full name. Everything that came up was old news, culminating with his death in prison ten years prior.

Next, she entered the name Cal Tovik on a whim. Then, she added the inmate status and death date, covering all her bases before she hit search.

The results were immediate.

Status: *Inmate*. Facility: *High Security* with the name of the prison her dad had been in. Date of death: *N/A*.

Tovik was still alive. Still locked away.

She exhaled her relief. It couldn't be her stepfather's old prison mate impersonating him under the name Viktor Renard, either.

The crease between Tommy's brows deepened. "Care to share?"

"Just checking a couple of theories. Neither is viable." She locked her screen and returned to staring out the window at the growing traffic.

"Whatever it is, you can tell me. You know that, right?"

She patted his arm. "I know. It's my brain finding a conspiracy at every turn."

"Hard not to right now. Seems to me some of our impossible ideas are valid, so don't hold back. I've got a few of my own."

"Let's hear them."

He wasn't fooled by her turning the focus on him. He humored her anyway. "If Dr. Wyn is working with Renard, she's our link to the Russian investors. I hate to say it, but I think we need to notify the swans and get the Agency to pick her up for questioning."

That he would suggest such a thing surprised her. She hadn't expected him to play it safe. To willingly turn over their investigation to Meg and the CIA. "They'll go after Renard, too, and Kaltrain. I'd like to get a look at the place and see if we can identify who's inside the Rover before we do that. If Renard or his friends get a whiff that the Agency is on their trail, they'll disappear, and we'll be no closer to bringing them to justice."

He nodded. "Wyn might clam up, too. We need the Justice Department to offer her a deal in exchange for naming Renard and the others in the plan."

Which would take a full confession on Tessa and Tommy's parts, followed by days, perhaps weeks, of red tape with the CIA, FBI, DOD, and others. It gave her a headache just thinking about it. "Balancing the safety of innocent people against bringing those responsible to justice is never an easy call. Our first goal should be averting disaster."

"Since the Agency already knows about the impending attacks, and Flynn has alerted the appropriate authorities, I'm not worried about that." His face was a mix of determination and the previous day's emotional turmoil. "I want to find Jessie and unravel what the hell is behind her faked death."

Tessa feared it wasn't something forgivable. And what would Tommy do, then?

Her mind trailed back to her stepfather. To the pieces of the names that kept intersecting with each other: Kaltrain—*Cal* Tovik. Tovik—a rearrangement of Viktor with an added R. Renard—meaning fox.

What in the covert world of intelligence was going on here?

She combed through her memories, dissecting all of those that surfaced. Her mother. Jessie. Her stepfather and his connections to the Agency.

The next few minutes passed in a haze. She barely noticed Tommy continuing to search and scan, putting more puzzle pieces together.

Thorough. She liked that about him.

Conscientious. She liked that, too.

What had passed between them the previous night and again this morning only added to her unease, though. She'd let him get under her skin.

The thought of him being hurt by all of this...

What game are you playing, Jessie?

A ferocious desire to protect Tommy filled her chest

and wormed its way into her heart. She nearly laughed at herself—when had she switched allegiances from Jessie to Tommy?

Traffic was a nightmare, slowing them to a crawl. "We're getting close," he said. "But at this pace, we'll lose them for sure."

Clarence's calm assurance came from the front. "Not to worry, sir. Lady Vulpe has a VIP registration at Heathrow with all the perks. We'll bypass the public areas, and I'll get you and m'Lady right to the dignitary and diplomat private access lanes."

Tommy shot her a grin. "M'Lady."

She punched his thigh. His hard, muscular thigh that only hours ago she'd run her hands, lips, and tongue over.

"Hey," he said, mock-angry. "Be careful, or I'll call you that all the time."

"Do so at your own peril."

He leaned over and put his lips against her ear. "Next time I get you naked, I'm at your service, *m'Lady*. Your wish is my command."

Well, when he said it like that... "I can be very demanding," she countered.

He nuzzled her neck, right below her ear. Goose flesh ran down her spine. "I look forward to it."

As they drew closer to Heathrow, the chaos of the airport intensified. Cars crawled slowly in every direction, taxis blared their horns, and travelers rushed with suitcases in tow. Clarence steered them smoothly into a less hectic lane, leading to the diplomatic drop-off.

Tommy sat forward sharply, pointing ahead. "There it is. The Rover."

The black Land Rover pulled away from the curb, merging into the stream of traffic.

"Follow it," Tessa ordered. "But keep a safe distance. We don't want them to suspect they have a tail."

Clarence maneuvered the SUV with practiced ease. The chase began, the Rover weaving through lanes and him matching its speed and shifts without drawing attention. Tessa gripped her door handle, her pulse racing. She wanted answers. *Needed* them. But, when the Land Rover gained enough distance to slip through a yellow light right before it turned red, they were stuck in traffic.

"Dammit!" Tommy slammed a fist against the seat. "We lost them."

"Not yet," Clarence said calmly, taking a sharp turn and bouncing over a sidewalk, sending several people screaming before he accelerated down a side street. "We'll catch them."

"What about your software?" Tessa asked. "Can't it show you where they are?"

Tommy shook his head. "Only when they stop. We would need a GPS tracker on the vehicle to watch it moving in real time." His head snapped up. "Wait a minute."

His fingers flew over the keyboard, whatever inspiration he'd had sending them into motion. Less than a minute later, he cackled, clapping his hands. "I hacked into the Rover's GPS."

Clarence gave him a smile in the rearview mirror. "Very good, sir. I'll let you direct me."

Tommy did, the two men acting like partners as he guided Clarence's driving from the rear seat. The streets grew quieter as they left the city's bustling heart behind. Soon, they entered Ilford, and it was no surprise when they cruised past skyscrapers of various heights and ended up in front of a modern one with a prominent sign announcing the headquarters of Kaltrain.

The Rover idled in a fire lane across the street from the main entrance. Several people walked past, paying no attention. The traffic light turned red, stopping them, and Tessa was thankful for the tinted security windows.

Both she and Tommy swiveled in the seat to watch as the Rover's passenger side door opened.

Her breath caught sharply in her chest like a fire—Jessie, pale but unmistakable, seemed to look right at her. The left side of Jessie's face was...not right. The cheekbone drooped, as did that corner of her lips.

But the second figure made Tessa's chest fill with a different fire—one of absolute fear.

"It's him," she whispered.

Tommy, mouth open as his gaze fixed on his sister, turned to her, alarmed. "Renard?"

She stared at the man. He took Jessie by the elbow and led her across the street, dodging cars, as he guided her to the Kaltrain entrance. Tessa's past crashed into the present like a meteor, scorching the entire foundation of her world. "His name is Harris Brewer. That's my stepfather."

SIXTEEN

The building loomed against the gray skyline, all sleek glass and sharp edges. A fortress for the powerful...and corrupt, Tommy suspected.

Tommy squirmed in his seat, his gaze locked on the entrance, where Viktor and Jessie had disappeared inside. Tessa sat stiff and silent beside him. After cruising around the block, Clarence parked across the street, close enough to watch the building but far enough not to draw attention. So far, no one had come or gone since the pair had entered.

Tommy wrestled with his emotions over seeing his sister. Wrestled with questioning Tessa about the man posing as Viktor, but whom she claimed was her stepfather. *The stepfather who had murdered her mother and been killed in prison?* Holy hell.

The ghosts of the past were indeed alive and creating nightmares. He exhaled slowly through his nose, fidgeting with the laptop. "I know you have a theory. Out with it."

Her hand tightened on her phone, her attention riveted on the imposing structure. "I wish I did."

"Come on, Tessa. Jessie's alive. Your stepfather's alive and posing as Viktor Renard. They're working together with the group behind the EMP attacks. What the hell is going on?"

She was already so stiff that he feared touching her might make her break apart. Yet, at his words, she stiffened further. Tommy wondered if she planned to stonewall him entirely.

Because he knew—*knew*—she was putting together the pieces of this puzzle. That's what The Architect did. She built theories and profiles the same way she designed buildings.

"Yes," she finally admitted, her voice barely above a whisper. "That's him. He's older, obviously, but I'd never mistake him for anyone else."

That was understandable, seeing as how he'd killed her mother.

"Jessie is working with him," she continued as if repeating it to herself would help her process it, "and they're running a widespread plan to destabilize US military bases and frame the swans—and by association—the CIA, for it. The design of such a plan is staggering. He must've been planning this for years."

Nerves clawed at him. "But why?"

"Revenge," she said without hesitation. "He must have believed The Agency would take care of him after he killed Mom. That he wouldn't end up in prison. His murder was staged, he escaped, and now he's seeking revenge."

"Which lets the CIA off the hook for faking his death," Tommy said. "If they'd played a part in it to get him out of prison, he wouldn't want revenge on them."

Working it through aloud, her body unfroze, and she nodded. "Someone he met in prison offered him an opportunity. Someone who had powerful connections in the outside world."

"Like our Russian investors?"

"Bigger, I imagine. A power player. Whoever it is, they discovered Harris had been a consultant for the CIA, and I'd bet that player has ties to the Russian government."

"FSB recruited Harris in jail?"

She nodded. "Them or one of their other undercover agencies. It makes sense."

A sleek silver Audi SUV stopped in front of the entrance. Several men in suits exited. A second vehicle pulled up behind them and out piled men in sunglasses and earbuds. From the bulge under their jackets, Tommy knew they were armed. *Bodyguards.* He raised his phone and snapped pictures of all of them as they entered the building.

"And who are these guests?" Tessa asked in a voice that sounded more like her—assured and in control.

"Let's find out," Tommy said, already uploading the photos to his software program. As he worked, Tessa toyed with her phone, seeming to debate whether to text or call someone. He knew what she was thinking—she wanted to put Spence or Del on tracking her stepfather's death. To alert them that he was alive and actively working on the EMP attacks, but doing so would require her to explain everything that had happened so far.

Despite the fact that she seemed back to normal, she wasn't. He knew the feeling. Her usual cool, detached, and logical brain wasn't functioning rationally. No matter how hard she tried to keep her emotions at bay, they were front and center.

Time for him to step up and offer her the support she'd given him the previous night when he'd been struggling with the impact of Jessie's manipulations. "This must be quite a blow."

Her chuckle was humorless, bitter. "Harris had this way of making people depend on him, even when they hated him. The piece of worthless—" She reared back and slammed her phone into the seat in front of her. It hit the leather and fell harmlessly to the floor as she raked both hands over her face, through her hair. Then she took a giant breath, and it was like she shut all the emotion down again. "I swear, Jessie looked right at me when she exited that vehicle. These windows are tinted. There's no way she could know we're inside."

He'd wondered the same thing but hadn't had time to sort it all out. "She followed us from Romania. She must've lost us when we switched from the train to the plane but figured out our destination, and that's why Renard—Harris—was picking her up at the airport."

"Which means that *he* knows we're here. At least he realizes we're in London."

Clarence, who had been silent, spoke up. "Perhaps it's unwise to stay in obvious view of the building."

"Give it another minute," Tessa told him. "Jessie must've picked up on our vehicle following them and assumed it's us—that we figured out she's alive or that her partner in crime is on our radar."

"Did you see her face?" Tommy asked. "The left side looks like it's... I don't know. Messed up. Scarred."

"Her cheekbone had been broken and didn't heal correctly." She hesitated a second, giving a slight head shake and staring out the window again, but seeming to see something else. "My mother had those kinds of injuries. Harris left significant damage and scars on her from his beatings. She would never go to the hospital, so some of them didn't heal properly."

Tommy's gut clenched. "Jessie was beaten and tortured."

Tessa seemed reluctant to confirm it but did with a jerky nod. "For all we know, she *was* kidnapped by Hagar, and it was his doing. At some point before the beheading, Harris stepped in as Viktor and traded her out. That's my guess."

His stomach twisted harder. He was no stranger to torture, but it was rare in his line of work behind a desk with computer code filling his head. The thought of Jessie enduring that kind of pain made his blood boil.

Tessa glanced at his screen, the program scanning the faces of the men who'd entered the building. "If Harris rescued her, that would explain why she's with him now. She might feel like she owes him her life."

"Top shelf manipulation," Tommy said.

Tessa retrieved her phone from the footwell. Across the street, movement at the entrance drew Tommy's attention once more. Two of the visiting guards had been joined by three others—probably Harris' team. They weren't average bodyguards—they had the hard look of mercenaries and the movements of highly trained former military personnel.

As one, they seemed to zero in on the Mercedes. Clarence's voice remained cheerful as he said, "It appears we have been spotted, m'Lady. Shall we make a hasty retreat?"

"Dammit," Tommy muttered, shoving his laptop onto the seat. "Drive, man!"

The SUV roared to life, pulling away from the curb just as the security team ran toward them. Tommy twisted in his seat, watching as the men pivoted, climbed into the pair of Audis, and began following.

Tessa chewed her bottom lip, also twisting to watch. "Clarence, you'll need to use some of that defensive driving."

"Understood," the man replied. "Let's see if they can keep up."

The next few minutes were a race of sharp turns, sudden stops, and narrow escapes as the butler with skills navigated the labyrinthian streets of Ilford. Tommy shifted between gripping the door handle, the back of the driver's seat, and Tessa's hand as they narrowly avoided collision after collision, darting between double-decker buses and jetting through red lights.

His adrenaline spiking, he felt the odd need to reassure Tessa. "You're right. Your driver is good. We'll lose them any minute."

Clarence caught his eye in the rearview, his patient grin in place. It seemed to say, *I told you so.* "We both want the same thing—to keep Ms. Vulpe safe."

Tommy clapped the man's shoulder over the back of the seat. "Her safety above all else, got it?"

"Must I remind you that I'm a trained CIA operative?" Tessa called over the squealing tires.

"Retired," Tommy corrected.

She met his eyes. Sheer determination shone in them. "Not anymore."

And, just like that, Contessa Vulpe was back in action.

He squeezed her hand as they rounded another corner to the blare of car horns. "Good," he said. "Time to kick some ass."

The next swerve caused her to tumble into his lap. He hugged her to him, providing a solid barrier between her and the door. "I've got you," he said.

THEY WERE BACK in the congested London streets before they lost their pursuers. "All clear," Clarence sang cheerfully, avoiding the main thoroughfares. "Shall we return to the castle?"

"Any chance Jessie knows about that place?" Tommy asked.

Tessa was still half in his lap. She didn't seem to be in a hurry to move away. "I've never talked about that part of my life with anyone, so no."

"What about your stepdad?"

"Since Mom gave up all rights to her inheritance when she was disowned by her family, it's doubtful. However, if he's run a background check on me, he may have found it."

"We can protect you," Clarence said. "And there's always Gryffindor. That's in my name."

"Gryffindor?" Tommy asked. "Like Harry Potter?"

"Long story," Tessa said. "Basically, grandfather willed his summer home to Clarence, and I've asked him to keep it well stocked in case I ever need it. It was named Gryffindor long before the famous wizard became one." She spoke to the chauffeur. "Take us to the castle. I need to think before I do anything else."

"Yes, m'Lady," he responded.

"Before *we* do anything else," Tommy corrected. "You're not in this alone."

They were pulling into the long drive when Tessa's phone rang. She glanced at it and froze.

"Meg?" Tommy guessed.

She blinked. "Blocked number."

Could it be Jessie? He grabbed the phone. "Let me answer it."

Her steely gaze met his, and she jerked it away. "No.

It's time for me to face this." She punched the button and put it on the speaker. "You've got thirty seconds to explain yourself."

But it wasn't Jessie.

"Hello, my little fox," a man's voice purred. "It's been far too long."

Tessa's sucked in a breath. She said nothing, then Tommy saw her icy control slip into place. "Not long enough, in my opinion. What do you think you're doing? You can't outsmart the CIA."

"Oh, Tessa, I think you know better than that. Come to me. We have much to discuss. Opportunities for you and the young Mendoza boy."

Tommy ripped the phone from her. "Not a chance, you bastard," he snapped. "Put my sister on the line."

Harris ignored him. "Tessa, don't make me come find you. You know I will. The consequences will be so... unpleasant."

Tessa let go of one of those emotionless chuckles. This one was edged with resolve. "Try it, you son of a bitch. I'll be waiting."

She disconnected, her hand shaking as she stared at the phone. Tommy knew she wasn't seeing it. She was lost in her memories.

"Let him come," he growled. "He'll learn a whole new meaning of the word 'unpleasant.'"

Tessa met his eyes, a stark fear quickly covered by that damn barrier she was struggling to keep in place. "This is my fight, Tommy."

He grabbed her by the back of the head and pressed a kiss to her lips. "Not anymore. He's going down, and I'm the one who's going to do it."

SEVENTEEN

Tessa entered the grand study, her voice echoing off the high ceiling as she issued orders to the staff. "Find every bulletin board in the castle, no matter how small. I need index cards, markers, and pushpins. Hurry."

Moda, Randall, and Clarence nodded, scattering to carry out her instructions. Although it was early fall, the London weather already made it feel like winter. The room was silent except for the soft crackle of the fire in the hearth.

Her mind turned over every detail and revelation swirling inside her brain in a chaotic storm. She pressed her fingertips to her temples, trying to force everything into order—Harris, Jessie, the suits that had shown up at Kaltrain, Dr. Wyn.

Tommy lingered near the massive desk, his arms crossed with a frown on his face. His gaze was fixed on her, a mix of concern and anger. Concern for her safety.

Anger at Harris. Uncertainty over Jessie. "You're sure we're safe here?"

"Relatively. For now."

"I need a weapon. Where do you keep them?"

She led him down the hall into a library of sorts. There, she ran her hand along a rugged tapestry covering half of the wall. She flipped the hidden switch, and behind the woven picture of a fox hunt, part of the wall slid aside. She held the tapestry so he could enter.

The weapons room was as impressive as the rest of the place. Tommy seemed impressed. "Whoa. You don't mess around."

"I've been on my own for a long time, Tommy. I'm always prepared."

She marched to a selection of handguns, loaded one of the Glocks, and shoved it in the waistband of her pants. It wasn't her favorite Sig, but it was a powerhouse anyway. "Help yourself."

He did, following her out a minute later with a shotgun and Glock. "I *will* protect you, you know."

Her laugh was little more than a sharp grunt as she closed the secret room. "I can handle whatever Harris throws at me."

"I know relying on someone doesn't come naturally to you, but maybe it's time you started believing you can rely on me."

She didn't answer. Couldn't. She stopped at an enclosed cabinet and opened the wooden doors to reveal a wall of monitors displaying the castle security feeds. With a few taps on the console, she expanded the view of the perimeter cameras. "If you intend to protect me, keep an eye on these."

She headed for the door. He stopped her, blocking her path. "You're not going to leave me here while you figure things out."

"We need to watch for unwelcome visitors. Either you do it, or I have to have one of the staff do it, which pulls them away from their posts at the entrances. Your call."

His lips firmed. "I can tap into the security feeds with your laptop and watch for Harris and his goons while I'm in the study with you."

A fissure of relief broke open inside her. She wanted him by her side, and if that made her weak, so be it. "Do it."

While he worked on that, she stepped away to make a call she dreaded. Flynn answered after two rings, his tone clipped. "Yeah."

"Always so professional when you answer your personal line."

"You bet your ass I am when people who don't work for me interrupt my workday."

She wanted to call him petty but decided she needed to get to the reason for this call. "Did you know?"

She heard someone in the background say something to him. He covered the phone and responded, then came back to her. "Know what?"

"About Harris."

There was more background noise, and she thought he must be walking down one of Langley's many hallways, encountering plenty of people who wanted his attention. "Who?"

She'd expected a deflection but not outright denial. Did he honestly not know? She wished she could believe that. He'd seen her personnel files. Knew everything about her. Harris had been a contractor long before Flynn even went to The Farm, but still... "If you're playing dumb, you'll regret it."

"I'm late for a meeting, so whatever this is about, spit it out, Vulpe. I don't have time for games."

"Neither do I. Look him up—Harris Brewer. He's behind the superconductor sabotage. He's working with Dr. Wynn at Cal Line. Harris Brewer is supposed to be dead, and he's using the name Viktor Renard as his alias." She laid out the rest, explaining the LLC and its connection to the Russian investors Tommy had uncovered. She didn't mention Jessie. "You've got a real problem on your hands, Director. I suggest you skip that meeting you're about to attend and put your brilliant mind to more pressing matters."

There was a long, calculating pause. "Where are you, Tessa? How did you discover this Harris fellow is behind all this?"

"I'll be in touch," she said and hung up before he could press further.

The staff returned with several bulletin boards and office supplies, piling them onto the table. Tessa set to work, her movements quick and precise. She scribbled notes onto the cards, each representing a piece of the puzzle: Harris' connection to the LLC shell companies,

Jessie's involvement, Mosai Hagar's role. The framework began to take shape but was still incomplete, riddled with gaps.

Tommy joined her, his handwriting a scrawl across more cards as he added what he knew. She felt his stare on her back as she kept rearranging the collection into different patterns, building out her stepfather's plan as if constructing the blueprints of a large, impressive structure.

The foundation. The frame. The facade. The space, form, and function of each element.

Moda entered with a tray of food and tea, setting it on the side table. "I already had this prepared. I'll take up my security point now," she said.

Tessa ignored her and the tray, her focus unyielding. Tommy glanced at the tray, then at her. "You should eat."

"Not now," she muttered, pinning another card to the middle board. "I'm onto something. I have to figure this out."

"Tessa," Tommy's voice broke through her thoughts.

She turned to see him holding a card with Jessie's name on it. "What if Harris didn't just use Jessie? What if he...?" He hesitated, then continued, "What if Harris did save her from Hagar?"

She turned that over, the idea that Jessie had done the wrong thing for the right reason. A form of Stockholm Syndrome—feeling indebted to the person who had kidnapped you. Hurt you. Forced you to commit crimes. "It doesn't absolve her of anything, even if he is manipulating her, but it fits more with the Jessie we knew."

Tommy chewed on a bite of sandwich. "But why? What does he gain from keeping her alive?"

"That's what we need to find out before it's too late."

Her phone buzzed, the screen lighting up with Meg's name. Tessa hesitated before answering, hitting the speaker button. "Made it to my place, I take it?"

"How could you?" Meg's voice sneered with accusation. "Are you with him now? Have you been sleeping with him all this time?"

Tessa flinched, setting her teeth and taking a breath before she responded. "Who?"

Tommy's gaze was once more boring into her back.

"You know who. *Tommy*." Meg was yelling now. "He was here. His fingerprints are all over the place."

"Fingerprints?" She gave a dry chuckle. "I see. So Flynn sent you to catch me in the act, did he? You guys suspected me all along. All that talk about needing me for the team... How could *you*?" she threw back. "I thought you wanted me to trust you."

"I did. I still do. But now? After this?" Meg made a disgusted sound. "Why? Why did you keep this from us?"

Dec came on the line. "What's going on, Tessa? Talk to us."

She shot Tommy a look that screamed, *I told you they'd figure it out*. "We have bigger things to worry about," she said.

"You lied to me," Meg snapped. "This whole time, you've been lying."

"Well, guess what? So has Jessie." She took a deep

breath to steady her nerves and forced calm into her voice. "She's alive, Meg. Jessie's alive."

Silence. Heavy, pregnant silence. "Have you lost your mind?"

Tessa explained her discovery, the revelation she and Tommy had made. Meg responded with more silence.

Tessa felt as if she might collapse into the chair next to Tommy. She leaned on the desk instead. "I haven't told Flynn," she said softly. "There's a lot I haven't told any of you."

Tommy gripped her hand, giving it a squeeze that encouraged her to let down her guard.

Handling a terrorist or crime lord here and there wasn't out of her skillset. Handling a massive planned terrorist plot that could affect the entire world? She needed a team. "How fast can you get to London?"

"What's in London?" Dec asked.

"Jessie," Tessa told them. She met Tommy's gaze, needing it to keep her vulnerability from overwhelming her. "We need to bring her home."

EIGHTEEN

She'd been waiting for the text or call since her discussion with the others the previous day. The only thing that had shown up was a drone.

Tessa had been quicker to the shotgun than Tommy. That was the only reason she'd been the one to blast it out of the air instead of him.

The message finally came as the midnight blue sky turned purple with the approaching sunrise.

Her phone vibrated on the nightstand, the soft buzz cutting through the stillness. She snatched it up and scanned the text.

We need to meet.

She replied, *Rose garden in five*, shutting off Tommy's alarm so the cameras wouldn't wake him.

She grabbed the shotgun resting near the back door. The castle was quiet, and its age-old stones and towering walls exuded a presence that both comforted and unnerved her. She stepped into the crisp night air, her breath faintly visible.

She made it with plenty of time to spare, Jessie taking longer than five minutes. Apparently, she'd been farther away than Tessa had assumed.

Jessie wore a thick jacket with the hood pulled up, her posture hunched. Tessa waited for her to approach, shotgun pointed at the ground but ready.

"You destroyed my favorite drone," Jessie said, her voice rougher than Tessa remembered. It wasn't just the tone but the cadence. Had Hager or Harris damaged her vocal cords?

"You destroyed your brother's life," Tessa shot back as she noted how much Jessie had changed. Her face was thinner, her jaw more defined. Even with the bulky jacket, Tessa could tell she'd lost weight.

"It wasn't by choice. Listen, you need to get Tommy out of here. Away from Viktor."

"His real name is Harris. Harris J. Brewer. He's my stepfather."

"I know. I also know he's a monster."

"Then why are you working with him?"

Her head dipped, the hood obscuring her features. "I have no choice."

"You always have a choice, Jessie." Tessa's voice cracked, betraying her anger. "You made all of us believe you were dead. Do you know the guilt Meg has carried for the past year? The guilt *all of us* have carried?"

Jessie's head snapped up. "It was either me or you," she whispered.

Tessa froze. "What?"

"He rescued me," Jessie continued, "but he said if I didn't do what he wanted, he'd kill Tommy."

That didn't answer her question, but it did confirm her theory. "Why did he need you?"

Jessie hesitated. "Because he couldn't have you."

Tessa's breath caught in her throat. She searched for another question, but her mind wouldn't form one.

Jessie took a step toward her. Tessa couldn't help it, she brought the shotgun up like a shield across her chest. Jessie stopped. "He's sick, T. He acts like I'm his daughter. He talks about how much he loves you and how you betrayed him. I'm your replacement. He watched us for years before he concocted this mythical family."

It took Tessa several heartbeats to process what Jessie was saying. Her grip on the gun tightened. "He killed my mother," she said, her voice cold as her pulse roared in her ears. "If anyone was betrayed, it was her. *Me.*"

Jessie's expression shifted to shock, guilt flashing across her face. "You never told me that." She took another tentative step forward, but Tessa continued to use the weapon as a shield and stepped back. "He says this is his legacy... That we're going to destroy the swans for what they did and remake the world power structures to prove his intelligence."

"What the *swans* did?" Tessa echoed. "What does that mean?"

"There was a mission in Syria a few years ago. We took down a group that was planning a cyberattack during the pandemic. It was more of a gray swan event, but the pandemic created all sorts of opportunities for men like Viktor—I mean, Harris."

"Let me guess, he was behind it."

Jessie nodded. "He and a team of hackers. He'd promised them millions. It all went belly up because we were sent into a political protest in Berlin that went wrong. Harris' hackers were killed. All of them."

In the back of her mind, Tessa prayed Jessie was telling the truth and this wasn't an elaborate misdirection. She scanned the gardens, the approaching dawn minutes away. Nothing seemed out of place. "Why didn't you come to me to begin with? Why did you let this go this far?"

Jessie's expression turned fierce. "Tommy is my brother. I look out for him. You don't have any siblings. You don't know what it's like. I will never put Tommy in danger. That's why I'm here. Viktor is always watching me—I have to get back. Please, T. Take Tommy and get as far away from here as possible."

"How soon before Harris sets off the EMP attack at the military bases?" Tessa pressed.

Jessie shook her head. "I don't know. Soon. He doesn't tell me specifics about his plan." She turned to leave, her movements jerky. "I have to go."

No message for Tommy? Tess's instincts sent up a red flag. "Tommy loves you so much. He doesn't want you doing this any more than I do."

Jessie stopped short, her back still to Tessa. "I know." She turned slightly and tossed something on the ground.

"Don't try to save me. Just... Tell Tommy I did this for him."

Tessa debated letting her walk away. It would be easy to cripple her, force her to stay. Her fingers flexed on the shotgun, the weight of the decision pressing down on her.

"Why don't you tell me yourself?" a ragged male voice said from behind Tessa.

Jessie didn't even hesitate. She threw something at Tessa, and suddenly, a dense cloud engulfed the garden around her.

Smoke bomb.

Tessa's eyes stung, and she coughed, swinging the shotgun around, but the world was a blur of gray.

She sensed Tommy racing past her, but by the time the smoke cleared, he and Jessie were gone.

NINETEEN

As he veered into the maze of roses, the scent of the blooms hung thick in the air. Thorns snagged at his sleeves, and his boots crunched on the gravel path. Ahead, Jessie's silhouette ducked behind a trellis. He surged forward, his breath steaming in the misty morning air.

Why is she running?

Stupid question.

A better one was, why the hell hadn't Tessa woken him up?

He'd deal with her later.

Ahead, Jessie slipped through a hedgerow. "Jessie!" he shouted.

From his left, two figures emerged from the shadows of a tree—Meg Carson and Declan Reid. Their weapons were drawn. They moved in tandem, joining him in the race to catch his sister.

"Where the hell did you come from?" he yelled at them.

"Finally decided to join the party, cub?" Declan teased.

He would've punched Dec in the face if they hadn't been in a race. "She's getting away!"

Meg's voice rang out. "Not for long." The sound of her gun going off made his insides drop.

Jessie tripped and went down. A sharp cry escaped her lips as she tried to scramble away from them, blood leaking from her calf. "You shot me!" she yelled at Meg.

"You shot her," Tommy echoed in distress. Now, he wanted to punch Meg.

He skidded to a stop, breathing heavily and staring down at Jessie. As she met his eyes, he saw a plea for forgiveness in them mixed with irritation over his pursuit. "Why couldn't you leave this alone?" she lamented.

"You're my sister!" He gripped her arm, firm but not brutal, and hauled her to her feet.

She couldn't put weight on the injured leg, hopping in place and leaning on him to steady herself. "Oh, Tommy. You have to let me go."

He couldn't help it. He hugged her, crushing her against his chest. Holding her again, smelling her hair, feeling her in his arms...it brought a tidal wave of emotions. "How could you leave me?"

She sobbed against his chest, her hands gripping the layers of his shirt. "You dummy. It wasn't about *leaving* you. It was about keeping you safe."

"Take her to the house." Tessa stood a few feet away,

watching the reunion with a cold, distant expression. The shotgun remained steady in her hands, though she didn't aim it at Jessie. Tommy felt her anger and disappointment over Jessie's actions boiling up with his, yet she kept hers contained. No matter Jessie's motivation, what she'd done had put all of them through hell.

Declan supported Jessie's weight on one side while Tommy did the same on the other. They marched her back to the castle, the sun peeking over the horizon and casting a pale orange hue on the gardens and rear door.

Inside the dining hall, Spence lounged in a high back chair, a porcelain teacup in hand. Steam rose in lazy spirals as he observed their entrance. "Well," he drawled, setting his cup down. His gaze roamed over Jessie like she was the best thing he'd seen in ages. "Our prodigal swan has returned."

Jessie glared at him and said nothing as they lowered her into a chair. Blood ran down her leg and onto the floor.

Tessa remained standing, the shotgun resting casually against her shoulder. Tommy inspected Jessie's wound while Meg paced and Declan leaned on the door frame.

Moda appeared, and Tessa sent her to retrieve first aid supplies.

"It's just a flesh wound," Tommy told him. He patted his sister's thigh. "You'll live."

Jessie sneered at Meg. "You always were the most accurate shot."

Declan cleared his throat. "Excuse me? Everybody knows I'm the sharpshooter on the team."

Meg and Spence exchanged a look. Spence tapped the screen of his phone and resumed sipping tea. "Recording now. Let's start from the beginning."

With her hood off, the deformity of her left side was more evident. Tommy tried not to stare.

"I'm injured," Jessie said.

"You're lucky it wasn't me who shot you," Tessa replied. "You'd be in far worse shape. Now, start talking, or I'll make you wish Meg had aimed higher."

Tommy shot her a warning glare. Tessa stayed neutral.

Jessie shifted uncomfortably and grimaced, hiking up her leg and putting pressure on her bleeding injury. "You don't understand. If Viktor finds out I've been here, he'll kill all of us. He'll set off the attacks and blame you for them."

"Blame us, how?" Meg asked. "What's his motivation for all of this?"

Tommy knew they needed the full details, but dammit, he was in Spencer's corner. He wanted Jessie to start from the beginning and explain what the hell was going on. He'd heard what she'd told Tessa in the garden, but he needed to have more facts rather than speculation.

Jessie's gaze swung to Tessa. "Did you pick up the USB I threw at you?"

Tessa withdrew the stick from her pocket and held it up. "What's on it?"

Before Jessie could answer, Tommy loomed over her. "Is it infected with a virus? Will it alert Harris?"

"No. Of course not," Jessie said. "Just look at what's on it. Everything you need to know is on there."

Reluctantly, Tommy accepted the drive from Tessa. By the time he returned with the laptop, Moda, the maid, had arrived with the bandages. While Tommy proceeded to take a few precautions before opening the drive, Spence appointed himself as medic and began to care for Jessie's wound.

As Tommy checked the background encoding, he was relieved there were no viruses. He began rooting through the files stored on it. "What is this?"

Tessa moved to peer over his shoulder. Jessie said, "It's Viktor's manifesto. His master plan. The proof he'll plant to frame the swans. Everything."

Meg joined them, standing on Tommy's other side as she read the screen. "We need to send this to Flynn ASAP."

"What's he going to do about it?" Jessie challenged, flinching as Spence used an alcohol wipe on her wound. "The moment Viktor gets wind of this, he can type in a code and set off those EMPs. Flynn won't even have time to blink. That's why you must let me go. We can't take the chance that he'll figure out I'm here or that I stole that information."

Tommy rubbed his eyes and returned to the document directory. "And this?" He clicked on a file labeled SWAN.

A series of files appeared, each bearing a team member's name. "What the hell?" Meg said as he selected the one with her name on it, and they scanned its contents. "This is... Everything about you," he said. "Your history, your skills, your missions. And it looks like details about your missions for Black Swan."

She scanned the material. "Fabricated details." She pointed at one of the entries. "That's not how the mission went down. We didn't have any contact with a Horace du Fossen."

Dec crowded in, also reading the screen. "I don't get it. What is this?"

"He wants to prove that the swans were never heroes," Jessie said. "That you've been the villains all along. He's setting you up to take the fall for the EMP attacks, and this evidence"—she emphasized the word— "is to prove that the swans have been *creating* the chaos that the CIA claims they're needed for. That they want to terrorize people so they can swoop in and save the day."

Dec grunted. "But we're ghosts. The public doesn't know we exist."

"Until Viktor broadcasts your identity to the whole world," Jessie countered, wincing again as Spencer wrapped her leg with gauze.

Tommy glanced at her. "Why would he do that?"

She looked tired, the kind of tired that sleep couldn't fix. "When I was first recruited for the team, I saw a memo written twenty years ago by a consultant for the Agency. It predicted a bunch of black swan events. The consultant's name had been redacted, and that memo was ignored. It mentioned the fact that the CIA should create a team like yours to handle such things, but apparently, no one took it seriously."

Spence finished and began packing up the first aid materials. He leaned a hip on the table. "What's that got to do with this, luv?"

"It was after Vienna." She glanced up at Spence, then addressed Meg and Declan. "There were too many coincidences about that mission. About the previous one, as well. It kept tickling my brain. I couldn't put my finger on it, but I felt like I'd seen, heard, or read about similar events. That's when I remembered that memo. I went digging for it, but it was gone. I had no way to figure out who the consultant was. I was out of luck."

Tessa un-cocked the shotgun, removing the shells and setting all of it on the table before slumping into a chair. "It was Harris. Or as you know him, Viktor."

"After he rescued me and forced me to work for him," Jessie said, "I found that manifesto in his files. He was so angry at being dismissed by the Agency that he decided to prove his point by creating the events himself."

Meg shook her head. "That's not possible. You can't create a black swan event."

"You can take advantage of a gray swan, though," Jessie argued, "and turn it into something far worse."

"Gray swan," Tommy murmured in thought.

"An event that can have severe repercussions on the economy but is unlikely to occur," Tessa said. "Like Brexit."

"I know what it is," he replied. He tapped his fingers

on the table. "A cyberattack on critical infrastructure must be his goal."

"Exactly," Jessie said. "He plans to make it look like you're all behind it." She spoke to him again. "He was so angry when he discovered you were onto him and the Russian investors. I tried to scare you off, but you—"

"Wouldn't quit," Tommy said. "And I'm not about to now."

"Why didn't you come to us?" Meg said. "Why didn't you tell me? Flynn? Someone?"

Her chin came up, defiant. "I was protecting my brother, and I couldn't risk Viktor—Harris— setting off those EMPs. I'm... I'm sorry." It was an apology for more than not sharing this intel sooner—it was for everything. "Please." She inched to the edge of the chair, pleading with them. "I have to go. He's probably already noticed I'm missing."

Tessa snatched up Spence's cup and downed the last of the tea. "You expect us to let you go back?" She snorted. "Fat chance."

"You don't have a choice," Jessie said, resolute.

Tommy admired his sister's confidence when she sat in a room full of people who would not give her any quarter.

"Maybe we do," Tessa said. "Sending you back to him might actually be the answer."

Tommy didn't like the calculating look on her face. "Where are you going with this?"

Tessa sized Jessie up. "You said he used you as a

surrogate for me. A stand-in. If he wants the real thing, I think we should give it to him."

Comprehension hit him at the same time it did Meg and the others. Meg nodded. Dec shook his head. Spence seemed to be considering the complications of such a plan but neither accepting nor discarding it outright.

"No," Tommy said. "Absolutely not."

"Hear me out." Tessa paced the length of the room. "Jessie will bring me to him. I'll let him think I'm willing to negotiate. We'll use it to get close and take him down."

Spence looked at his empty cup. "A Trojan horse. We send you in and strike from the inside."

Jessie shook her head. "It won't work. He's too paranoid."

"He called me and told me to come to him," Tessa countered. "He wants me to see how brilliant he is."

"It might work," Meg said.

"You can plant a virus to infect his computers with," Spence added. "I can send it with you. We can disrupt the attacks before he can set them off."

"No," Tommy said again, more insistent this time. He shook his head at Spence, Dec, and Meg. "He's a murderer. An egomaniac. A tyrant. You're not letting her walk in there."

"*Letting* me?" Tessa's voice had a brittle edge to it. "I'm doing it. This is our best bet. End of discussion."

Tommy stared her down. "Not without me, then. I'm going with you."

Jessie used the table to help her stand. "None of you are listening. *It won't work.*"

Tessa faced her. "Let's get something straight, Jessie. You're in no position to hand out orders. While you may have critical intel, you don't get a vote in how we proceed."

Jessie glanced at each of them.

"You owe us," Meg said. "Stop this madness. Help us bring him down."

Jessie was quiet for a long moment, seeming to search for another argument. Tommy held his breath until she whispered, "Fine. What do you want me to do?"

"The swans ride again," Spence said, a bit too cheerily for Tommy's liking.

"I'm *not* a swan," Tessa reminded him.

"Screw that," Meg said. "You are, too." She glanced at the open doorway. "Now, how do we get some breakfast around here? We have a full day ahead of us."

TWENTY

Tessa stepped into the cavernous halls of Kaltrain's headquarters, her stomach a knotted mess. Jessica's hand was on her elbow, her grip tight, even though she'd zip-tied Tessa's wrists. They'd agreed to a compromise, but Jessie was flat-out sure their plan was going to fail.

"I hate this," she murmured.

Tessa reined in the scream that kept clogging her throat. "I hate that you betrayed all of us and nearly ruined your brother emotionally."

"I told you why," Jessie ground out.

"While protecting your brother at all costs may be a valid reason for doing the unthinkable in certain situations, your reasoning in this case is irrational. The result of your actions put him in more danger than coming clean would have. And that's why we're here—his well-being is now *my* responsibility because you're no longer competent to handle it."

Jessie grunted. "I hate you right now," she snarled.

"Get over yourself. And by the way, Tommy's a lot stronger than you give him credit for. Your death nearly killed him, too. You're lucky he's forgiven you."

"Oh, and you know him so well. I'm his big sister. I've been taking care of him my whole life."

She had to play this right. Every move, every word, every gesture would be scrutinized and dissected by those behind the cameras. "He's not a kid anymore, and neither are you," she said under her breath. "You're playing an exceedingly dangerous game, and no matter the outcome, Tommy's the one who will pay the price."

"No." Jessie shook her head. "This is all on me."

Wishful thinking.

The overhead canned lights cast a sterile, surgical glow over the polished concrete floors. They bypassed a receptionist, who gave Jessie a nervous glance. "Mr. Renard is not to be disturbed."

"He'll want to be disturbed for this," Jessie snapped.

The woman snatched up her phone and punched a button.

At the elevators, Jessie whispered, "Remember, there's a guard outside the entrance to Harris' penthouse suite and one just inside the receiving area where he conducts business. He'll be in his inner suite, where no one is allowed. Cherie back there is alerting him to the fact I've returned and brought company. We might make it past the guard stationed at the outer door of the penthouse, but no farther than that."

The security cameras were invisible, but Tessa could feel watchful eyes on them. If her stepfather were as conniving as he appeared, his team would already have her identity. Making it past his security would be easy—he'd be anxious to talk to her. "Relax. I can handle him."

"He's a snake with wicked venom. Relaxing lands you six feet under."

Point taken. The elevator doors slid open with a soft *whoosh*. Inside, the two of them said nothing, and Tessa kept her expression cold and remote. Jessie didn't remove her grip, her nails digging into Tessa's skin through her jacket.

She was understandably nervous. They both were. But Tessa locked down her fear and anger—emotions would only impede her end goal.

As predicted, the first guard at the penthouse door didn't pull a weapon or insist they leave. He nodded at Jessie and patted Tessa down for weapons before he opened the door. Jessie strode inside, tugging Tessa by her bound wrists with her, right past the interior guard, who had to weigh close to three hundred pounds and looked down on them with disdain.

Tessa wasn't sure how to react when she saw her stepfather. She expected Harris to be seated at an impressive desk, cocky and impertinent, sure that she would obey his commands.

While his massive black desk drew the eye to the center of the room, he stood in front of a set of floor-to-ceiling windows behind it. Feet braced, a drink in one hand, he stared out the impressive windows at the street below with an air of palpable self-importance.

His profile showed he had aged considerably, with

deep lines bracketing his lips and eyes. His hair was white. The side of his mouth quirked in a smile—the only acknowledgment of their entrance. "Where have you been?"

Tessa wasn't sure if he was speaking to her or Jessie. Jessie answered. "Hunting her down." Her voice was devoid of anything but resentment and pique. "Where did you think I was? You said you wanted her, so I brought her to you."

He swirled the liquid in his glass, took a sip, and heaved an aggrieved sigh. "Unnecessary. She would have come on her own, wouldn't you, my little fox?"

His voice...the stuff of nightmares. Tessa locked her knees and remained impassive even though her body trembled.

Keeping one hand on his hip, he strolled to his desk. The bold modern lines matched him with their commanding presence. He didn't so much as glance at her, setting down the glass and sliding some files aside before he sat, leaning back and steepling his fingers in front of him.

His gaze tracked up her pants, jacket, and tied wrists as if he were sizing her up inch by inch. She gritted her teeth. When his focus landed on her face, he continued to take her in one piece at a time—her chin, her mouth, cheekbones, and nose. Her left ear, then her right. Her hair. When his eyes finally met hers, the lines around his mouth deepened as he gave an exaggerated frown. "You look just like your mother."

Pure scorn in those words. His body was tense, even though he tried to hide it. That condescending frown...

She remembered it—the one that said he wanted to hit something. Some*one*. Her own body cramped in an instinctive response. Her stomach roiled.

Clamp it down. She would not become that cowering child again. The one who couldn't help her mother, even though she tried. The girl who had attacked him on more than one occasion when he was beating her mom, only to end up bruised and broken alongside her.

The grown, take-no-shit woman she was now flooded her system. She almost wanted to egg him on. To challenge him and see if he would come across that desk after her. She wasn't a weak little girl anymore. She knew moves that could bring him to his knees.

Jessie nudged her forward.

Even with her resolve, she stumbled as she ended up closer to him. Only a few feet separated them. His cologne and the smell of his liquor penetrated her nose.

Suddenly, she wanted to do more than bring him to his knees—she wanted revenge for her mom. "You look just like the bastard I remember," she said with false calm. "Only older and uglier."

He came up out of his chair, and she braced, ready for the punch she knew was coming. He gripped his glass instead, shooting down the last of the liquid and slamming it back down.

She didn't wait for his next move, taking charge of the interaction. "Instead of trading insults, let's get to it. I'm ready to offer you a deal." She left the carrot dangling, proud that her voice was steady.

He hid his surprise well, but she saw a flash in his eyes before he forced himself to relax and smirked. "You're offering *me* a deal?"

"I know what you're planning, and I want to offer my expertise," she said simply. "You'll also get my silence."

There were always two sides to any deal. "In exchange for?"

"Jessie's freedom."

"What?" Jessie stepped up beside Tessa, giving her a shocked expression before turning it on Harris. "That's not why I brought her here. I did it for you."

He made a dismissive gesture, and Jessie, being the good little pawn, stepped back again. He focused on Tessa. "You're not walking out of here, Contessa. I've already got your silence, and I can force you to do whatever I want. Letting Jessie go would be stupid. Because of your friendship, she offers the perfect leverage to keep you in line. No deal."

So cocky.

She saw the mental calculations churning in his mind. Good. Let him think he had the upper hand. "You may be a bastard, but I thought you'd at least make a deal in good faith with me since I allowed her to bring me in."

Jessie harrumphed. "*Allowed*? I abducted you right out from under Tommy's nose. Give me some credit."

"You were always a decent student, Jess, but not my equal by any means. I'm here because I want to be, not because you forced me."

Jessie's eyes widened artfully. Harris chuckled.

Tessa leaned forward as if Harris *were* her equal and she wanted to share a secret with him. "You've built something remarkable, and I'm no fan of the CIA or the Black Swans. I'm sure you know that. But even the best plans have weaknesses. Blind spots. I'm offering to help you eliminate yours."

"You want more than Ms. Medoza's freedom," he said, catching on.

"I know an opportunity when I see one."

He resumed his seat, rocking back and forth with his fingers steepled again. Those intrusive eyes bored into her. "What weaknesses do you think I have, little fox?"

I, he'd said, not *we*. Not *my plan*. He was taking it personally. Another plus for her. "Pursuing revenge creates a narrow focus. Your inner demons get the best of you. You get sloppy, predictable. Patterns emerge. Just like when you used to beat up Mom—you followed your right hook with a left uppercut." She tapped a finger on the desk. "Every. Time."

His face blanched. He rocked a bit more aggressively. "You think you know me, Contessa?"

She did. Too well. "Nothing surprises me anymore. Nothing escapes my notice. While you laid breadcrumbs to put the Agency in fear of an EMP attack on military bases, you've been working on far more while they're distracted with that, haven't you? Revenge is what you're after."

"Power is what I seek."

"That's what you tell yourself."

He glared. She glared back. A standoff ensued. She knew the first one to talk lost this game of wills.

It wouldn't be her.

He stood, ambling to the windows again, bracing his hands against the sides of the metal frames and staring at the scene before him. She wondered if he saw any of it or was inside his head, moving the pieces on his mental chess board around to see which would get him what he wanted.

But she'd hit her target, letting him know his plan wasn't so secret. That she knew he wanted to expose the Black Swan Division and paint them as terrorists inside their own organization. Cripple the Agency. Get them tangled up in congressional hearings and a media frenzy that would land certain members of the upper echelon in prison for treason.

"Your loyalty is to the CIA," he said flatly.

She breathed a silent sigh. He'd spoken first. She had him on the hook. "My only loyalty is to myself. You taught me that."

He peered at her briefly before returning to the view. "I don't believe you."

"Yet, here I am. Despite what Jessie believes, I willingly walked in here and am offering to help you. Don't you get it? I don't want to stop you. I want to help you bring down the swans and the Agency. They've kept me on a leash even though I walked away. I want my freedom."

Boldly, she went around the desk and plopped down into his chair, kicking her feet up onto the corner of the black monstrosity. Everyone in the room jolted as if shocked.

The security baffoon strode toward her.

Harris held up a hand to stop him.

Tessa cocked her chin at Jessie and the guard. "I'm not saying anything else until they're gone. Her loyalty lies with her brother, and although she's been useful to you so far, you won't need her any longer. Do we have a deal or not?"

Harris flared his hands outward. "I can't simply let her walk out. She knows too much."

She tapped her temple. "Blindspot, right there. She knows that if she talks, Tommy will die." She gave Jessie a stern, condescending glower. "That's a promise, Mendoza. If you want to protect your brother, keep your mouth shut."

Jessie stepped forward, matching her in intimidation. "Don't you dare threaten him."

Tessa smiled at her stepfather. "See? She'll do anything to keep the brat safe. Tommy is her blindspot."

Harris stood for a long moment, holding eye contact with Tessa. She saw something behind his cold, calculating gaze shift. He was logical above it all, and everything she'd told him fit with his warped belief system. He motioned at Jessie. "Go downstairs. I'll speak to you when we're done here."

Tessa didn't dare glance away. Another test. Another game. Jessie gave a dramatic sigh and stomped for the door. "You can't trust her," she said to Harris. "She's *your* blind spot. Don't say I didn't warn you."

When the door closed behind her, he smiled at Tessa. "Time to prove yourself."

She shrugged. "What do you want me to do?"

"Help me bring down the CIA, of course."

Tessa returned her feet to the floor and stood, snagging a glass paperweight and toying with it. Jessie would now be on her way to the server room with the USB Tommy had given her.

Tessa needed to buy her time. Keeping her stepfather's attention on her and feeding his ego might encourage him to divulge more than he intended.

"I admire your ambition," she said, shoving the stack of papers aside and finding a prize for her efforts. Carefully, with her body shielding her movements, she slipped the letter opener into her pocket before sitting on the edge of the desk. She continued to play with the glass paperweight. Nothing more than a magician's trick to keep Harris distracted. "But ambition without precision is risky. Your plan has too many moving parts and too big of a scale. Without a solid foundation, it will fall apart."

He bristled. "Risk is the price of progress."

"Do you want my professional opinion or not? If all you want is someone to lick your shoes, bring Jessie back. I'm here to pick apart your plans and help you rebuild something more reliable. More satisfying."

He stepped closer, looming over her and jerking the paperweight from her hand. The monster behind the slick suit and the overconfident ego slid to the surface. "Satisfying how?"

She'd guessed right—vengeance was still the bottom

line. "Don't you want to ensure your legacy is unassailable? To create something so flawless that no one could ever challenge it?"

The monster grinned. "Such as?"

"Are you willing to listen and do what I say?"

"I want everyone to know who I am, and I want to bring down the world so it grovels at my feet."

"Then don't waste my talents. I'm here. I care nothing about the Agency, so let me handle them. We need to put you to work on something bigger."

He grabbed her chin and held her face in place as he studied her. The promise of violence was in his eyes. The feel of his cold fingers on her skin made her gut clench. Her earlier meal threatened to come back up. She held her breath, running through her options to maim him should he strike.

His grin turned pleased. That's what he wanted—to put her in fear of him again.

With that smug smile, he released her and opened one of his desk drawers. When she saw what he withdrew, her blood ran cold. A knife.

But all he did was use it to cut through the zip tie, freeing her wrists. Tossing the knife down, he walked to a door at the far end of the room. He didn't look back.

She followed, her pulse erratic.

And found herself inside Harris Brewer's inner sanctum.

Time for phase two.

Unbeknownst to him, the rest of the team was inside the facility. By now, Meg and Dec should have infiltrated as maintenance workers, their uniforms and forged IDs allowing them access to critical areas. Tommy would be in the control room, monitoring the building's systems and preparing to override them at a moment's notice when Jessie gave him the signal. Spence was stationed nearby, ready to activate the Trojan horse Jessie was planting via the USB.

Every move was coordinated. Every contingency was accounted for. This is what Tessa did: design operations that prepared for every variable, every possibility.

Harris didn't offer her a seat, and she didn't take one. For the next few minutes, she continued to play on his ego and let him gloat about his supposed invincibility, asking a few questions here and there to keep him talking. As he did so, she offered suggestions for tweaking the plans he had in place to create something bigger and better.

And then, just when she thought she had him convinced of her sincerity, he chuckled. "Clever. You always were clever."

He rose from his chair, moving to a small cabinet, where he retrieved something she couldn't see. Returning to her, she realized too late that it was a pair of metal handcuffs. He locked one around her wrist and the other to the chair arm before she could protest.

She yanked against the restraint. "What are you doing?"

His fist came at her jaw before she could duck. She went sprawling to the ground, taking the chair over with her. Stars danced in front of her eyes, pain radiating up into her skull.

He stood over her, and she tried to scoot away before he could kick her the way he always had her mother once he got her down on the floor. Too late, he stomped a booted foot into her kidney.

She cried out, more from shock than pain, but shifted to grab his ankle. He lost his balance, tumbling into the edge of the desk. She forced herself to her feet, lunging at him.

The chair made it awkward, and he batted her away. She fell over the piece of furniture, landing on the floor, but as he came at her, she used her momentum to jerk the chair up and jammed the end of a leg into his stomach.

He bellowed, anger driving him to rush her again. She blocked him with the chair back. He snatched it from her grasp, wrenching her arm hard and slamming the edge of it down on her.

The air whooshed out of her lungs. She tried to roll away, but he kept his grip on the chair, pinning her in place.

His fist was a brick that smashed into her cheek. The second swing broke her nose.

He raised his fist to strike a third time. She screamed, and the room plunged into darkness.

TWENTY-ONE

The sound of Harris striking Tessa froze Tommy's blood.

He couldn't wait for the signal they'd agreed on. Couldn't stick to the timeline or trust the Trojan horse to do its job. Harris had her, and that bastard had no boundaries.

Fingers flying over the keyboard, Tommy hammered out a series of commands. The lights flickered once, twice, then went dark. The hum of the servers ground to a halt as his work took out the primary electrical grid.

The backup generator sputtered, struggling to engage. It wouldn't succeed. Tommy's virus had burrowed deep, ensuring there would be no power to salvage.

The darkness cloaked him as he shoved the chair aside, sprinting out of the security room and toward the stairwell, slipping on his night vision goggles.

He took the concrete steps two and three at a time, heart pounding. His legs, fueled by adrenaline and a sharp edge of panic, flew up and up, story after story. He replayed Tessa's voice in his head, steady, even as he knew Harris had intimidated her. She had the bastard where she wanted him. The Architect was running the show, but the stakes were unbearable.

She'd warned him. Warned all of them that this would happen. No matter what they heard, they were not to charge in and stop what was happening. She had it under control.

He couldn't follow those orders. Tessa was alone with a deranged madman.

He hit the top floor. The fire door flew open as he slammed into it. The guard outside the main door to the penthouse was jiggling the locked handle and calling to the guard on the other side. At the sound of Tommy approaching, he wheeled around, his flashlight beam catching Tommy in the face.

When he saw Tommy bearing down on him, he reached for his weapon, but Tommy was there before he could pull it out.

Two swift blows, and the man was unconscious at his feet. Tommy confiscated the gun and stuck it in the back of his waistband. At the door, he listened. The guard on the inside had gone quiet.

The voice inside his head, urging him on, mixed with the unease in his stomach. With the Glock in one hand and a Taser in the other, he fired the gun at the doorknob. It blew apart in chunks, and he kicked it open.

The security guard inside fired, and a bullet barely

missed his shoulder. He zapped the giant of a man with the Taser, and the ground shook when he hit the floor.

After a quick scan, Tommy felt a new rush of panic. Light from the windows illuminated the space, so he shoved the night vision goggles up on his head. Where was Tessa? Where was Harris?

The inner sanctum. Of course. He tossed the stun gun down and was moving toward the door at the end of the room when it flew open. Tessa staggered through it, Harris behind her with a gun pointed at her head.

He had her in a choke hold, his arm around her neck. "Tommy, isn't it?" Harris said in a mocking tone. "Playing hero, I see."

Jessie rushed in, a flashlight in hand. The beam spotlighted Tessa and Harris. Blood trailed from Tessa's nose and a split lip. Despite what had to be obvious pain, her eyes burned with fury. Tommy wasn't sure if it was directed at Harris or at him and Jessie for defying her orders.

"Drop your weapon, Harris," Tommy ordered. "Let her go. It's game over for you."

Jessie raised her weapon. A smile curled Harris' lips. "The loyal brother. I know all about you, kid. You have no idea how outmatched you are right now." He rubbed the side of his face against Tessa's. "Tell him, little fox. Tell your plaything how outmatched he is."

"Outmatched?" Tommy barked a laugh. "Your comms are down. Your servers are fried. Your guards? Neutralized. My team is in place, and Director Flynn—

you remember him—has been recording every word you've said."

Harris' smile faltered, but his grip tightened on the gun. "You think cutting the power matters? You think this...hero move changes anything? I've already won, idiot. My superconductors are everywhere. I'll bring down the energy grids, the military. Crash the stock markets. You've got your sister, why don't you go play and let the big boys get back to work?"

"Tommy's right," Jessie said. "You're done. Your plan failed. Let my friend go."

"My favorite swan," Harris mocked. "Contessa is right, you know? You're good, Jessica, but my daughter is a genius. The missions she worked during her time with the CIA—the scheming, cunning, manipulating. Ah, yes. A thing of beauty, the way her mind works. It's because of me, you know. I taught her how to survive. How to find her enemy's weakness and exhort it. You and your brother are idealists. Weak and sad. I could have given you the world if you'd understood the difference between people like us and people like yourselves."

"It's over," Tommy said. He tried to keep eye contact with Harris and not get distracted by Tessa's brutalized face and the way she seemed to be drawing into herself, growing smaller right in front of his eyes. Losing that inner light that he'd come to admire and love. "Let. Her. Go. Or I'll drop you where you stand."

Harris sneered. "I'm the solution to the chaos in the world. The energy crisis, the wars... I can fix it all. I'll create order out of the fall of governments and institutions. I am the ultimate black swan. Don't you get it?"

"You're a megalomaniac with a god complex," Tessa whispered. She spit blood on the floor. Tommy almost whooped with joy. The woman he knew was back. "Like most megalomaniacs, you're also delusional. You're just another petty tyrant, tearing things down because you didn't get hugged enough as a kid. A weak man who uses his fists to try and empower himself. There isn't one thing that's special about you, Harris. Men like you are a dime a dozen."

His face contorted into a monster. His grip around her neck tightened, causing her eyes to bug out. "The world has never seen a man like me." He forced the end of the gun deeper against her temple. To Tommy and Jessie, he said, "We're walking out of here. If you try anything, she dies."

Tommy froze. Jessie's gaze darted to him.

Tessa's gaze met his. Her fingers dug into Harris' arm, tugging at it to relieve the pressure on her windpipe. "Let...us...pass..." she ground out. "I...want...to go...with him."

Tommy realized what she was doing—positioning herself for one final play.

Harris smirked. "Of course you do." He rubbed his lips against her hair, drawing a deep breath as if scenting her shampoo. "You're still my girl."

Tommy wanted to bellow. He was going to break every bone in the man's body.

Jessie laid her weapon on the desk and backed away to clear a path to the door.

"You, too, kid," Harris said to Tommy. "Get out of my way."

Tessa gave him a ghost of a smile as Harris' arm loosened around her neck.

Swallowing past his rage, Tommy mimicked his sister's actions, laying his weapon next to hers and giving Harris a wide berth.

Harris nudged Tessa forward, gun still at her temple. "If you change your mind," he said as they moved for the exit, using Tessa as a shield, "I'm sure my daughter here will find a place for you in our new world order after we watch it all burn."

Tessa moved so fast that Tommy almost didn't realize what she'd done. Harris gasped and doubled over. The gun fired. Tessa fell to the floor, Harris on top of her.

His gun skittered across the floor. Jessie was on it, snatching it up as Tommy brought out the one in his waistband and bore down on Harris.

Who gasped for breath. Tommy yanked him off Tessa and saw blood staining his suit where a letter opener had been embedded between two of his ribs by Tessa.

The man continued to gasp like a fish out of water. She'd punctured a lung.

Tommy punched Harris in the face because, damn it, he didn't care if the asshole was two steps from Hell's gates, he deserved that and so much more. Then he shoved him at Jessie, who propped Harris against the desk, zip-tied his wrists, and called in their backup.

Tommy kneeled beside Tessa, who lay unmoving. The wool carpet had turned red on her right side, blood gushing from between her fingers where she pressed a hand against a wound. "Told you..." she said, her face pale and eyes glazing over, "I had it handled."

Panic clawed at his chest. "Spencer," he roared in his comm. "We need an evac now!" He stripped off his jacket and shirt, balling the cotton material up and using it to cover the gunshot wound. She winced and cried out, and he eased up, but only slightly. There was so much blood. Too much.

"Game over," she whispered, her words slurring.

"Shh," he said, the panic all-consuming. "You're going to be fine. Swear on my life, I will not let you die."

Meg and Declan burst in, saw Tessa on the floor, and exchanged a horrified glance. "Ambulance is on the way," Declan told him.

Meg holstered her weapon and fell to her knees on the other side of Tessa. Spence burst in, took in the scene, and swallowed hard. "Hey, luv," he said to Tessa. "You're getting sloppy if you let that bugger shoot you."

She shot him the finger.

He smiled. Tommy snarled at him. Spence's smile faltered, and he made his way to Jessie. The two of them embraced and murmured in low voices.

Flynn's goons arrived, arrested Harris, and a medic ordered Meg and Tommy away from Tessa. Tommy refused to go far, but Tessa gave him the side-eye, and he gave the medic enough space to work. A second one administered help to Harris, and when he was wheeled out on a stretcher, he cast a forlorn glance at Tessa. "Stupid girl," he wheezed. "We could have...had it all."

She shoved the medic aside and sat up, grimacing. "You want to know what your biggest weakness is? Underestimating others. You underestimated me, and that's a mistake you won't live to make again."

"You can't stop me," Harris panted.

Tommy started to slam his fist into the man's face again, but Declan stopped him. The bastard was wheeled away, and Tommy and Declan got Tessa on a second gurney. "I can walk," she protested.

The EMT snorted, sticking a piece of latex across the IV needle she'd inserted into Tessa's arm. Jessie held the bag of fluids. "Sure you can. How about you let me—"

Tessa weaved her fingers through Tommy's and hauled herself onto her feet. She swayed, and he caught her. "Listen to the medic," he chastised. "You've lost a lot of blood."

"I'm not letting that asshole get the best of me. I can and will walk out of—" Her eyes rolled up in her head, and Tommy caught her as she fell.

He lifted her into his arms, jutting his chin toward the open door. "Let's go," he said to their group.

And he carried her to the waiting ambulance outside, praying every step of the way that she didn't die on him.

TWENTY-TWO

Tessa came up from the depths of a floating sensation to waves of pain. Dull, but still enough to make her curse inside her head.

The sterile hospital room came into focus in pieces—first, the soft beeping of the heart monitor, then a dim light from a nearby window. The faint smell of bleach and the stiff feel of sheets. Beige walls, ugly curtains, the weight of a warm hand wrapped around hers.

"Welcome back," Tommy said.

Her brain and body felt sluggish and exhausted, but his voice...oh, that deep, confident voice she loved so much, made the instant panic fluttering in her chest stop.

She turned her head just enough to see him sitting beside her. His shirt was dirty, wrinkled, and stained with blood. Hers or his? His hair was disheveled, reminding her of the mornings she'd woken to see him next to her in bed. Dark circles bruised the area under his eyes, but his smile was bright.

"What happened?" she croaked, her throat dry.

He brought her a glass of water from the side table and guided the straw to her lips. "Easy. You've been out for a while."

The water was cool and soothed her throat. After a long drink, she leaned back against the pillow. Her memories returned, bringing that old, familiar sense of dread. "Harris?"

Tommy's grin faltered. He hesitated long enough for her stomach to drop. "You hurt him good, T, but he escaped. They brought him here for treatment, and somehow, he managed to evade the watch they put on him."

Her heart sank. The panic spread.

Tommy squeezed her hand. "Meg, Declan, and Spence are on his trail. He won't get far in his condition."

But he was out there. Free. Her bottom lip trembled, and she bit it to hold back angry tears.

"We disabled the EMPs, saved the bases, and exposed him," Tommy said. "The CIA, in conjunction with several other agencies, has shut down the Russian investor group and frozen all the funds tied to every LLC and shell company Harris touched. He has no cards left."

If only she could believe that. "And Jessie?"

"At Langley being debriefed by Flynn and some others. She's got a lot to explain, but she'll be all right. I've got her back."

Tessa nodded. "I'll do what I can to support her, too, even though I'm still upset with her." She would do it for Tommy. With Jessie's insight into her stepfather's strategies and contacts, Tessa might figure out where he'd gone and what he might try next.

But the weight it all felt like a thousand-pound elephant on her chest. Her side ached. Her eyes felt heavy. A gnawing question in her mind insisted on an answer. "What will you do now?"

Tommy's grin returned, softer this time. "Jessie and I have some catching up to do. Flynn's offered me a spot on the swans."

How was it possible her stomach could sink any lower? "What?"

He shrugged, nonchalant. "Apparently, they need someone like me to fill a vacancy. Since you've refused to take the position—"

"I've earned that spot," she argued, struggling to sit up straight despite the protest from her side.

Tommy didn't try to help her, chuckling as he leaned back in the chair and crossed his arms. "Guess you better get well enough to fight me for it, then, Vulpe."

It hit her then—what he was doing. The sneaky SOB. She rolled her eyes and settled herself into the pillows once more. "I'm clearly the better operative."

"Is that so?" His tone was teasing, but his gaze was steady and warm. It was also entirely too knowing. Unnerving. "You said you didn't want the job. In fact, correct me if I'm wrong, but you've done everything in your power to avoid being a swan."

Ire rising, she steeled herself against the pain and fog, swinging her legs over the edge of the mattress. "Flynn needs me to hunt down Harris since he was an idiot and let him escape. I don't care if they call me a swan, or The Architect, or a dog on a bone, I'm not sitting this one out." And when she caught Harris this time, she would ensure he never took another breath. Never hurt another person. If meting out justice like that made her a vigilante and a horrible person, then so be it. She would live with the consequences of her actions and never regret them for one moment.

Tommy shot out of the chair, putting his hands on her shoulders to keep her from standing. "You're not going anywhere. Doctor's orders."

She knocked his hands away. "I don't need your permission, and I could care less about the doctor's orders."

"You are so stubborn," he said, exasperation and affection blending seamlessly into his voice. Without warning, he shifted her farther back on the bed and climbed in beside her. He settled his weight enough to pin her in place without hurting her.

"Tommy! What the hell?"

He smirked in her face, his lips close enough to kiss. "If you think I'm letting you out of this bed in your condition, you've got another thing coming."

"Now, who's being stubborn?" she challenged, trying to keep the anger stirred up enough inside her to fight him. Looking into his eyes, seeing that smirk, she couldn't. "You're insufferable."

"True," he said, his gaze dropping to her swollen lip. He touched it with one of his knuckles, brushing it gently. "But you need me, and I'm not going anywhere."

That stubborn part of her bristled at the thought of needing anyone. Of leaning on him. He'd already gotten past her defenses more than once, and now he was doing it again. She tried rebuilding the walls she'd kept so carefully constructed until he'd shown up on her doorstep, but as fast as she slammed the bricks into place, they crumbled.

Maybe she could blame it on the drugs pumping through her system or the trauma she'd just survived, but she had the urge to kiss him.

She *did* need him, dammit.

And wasn't that a fine pickle to be in?

"I don't need you," she told him, lying through her teeth, "but I want you. There's a difference."

He chuckled. "Not to me."

Oh, this man! He frustrated her at every turn. "You're ridiculous," she murmured.

And then she tugged on his wrinkled and bloody shirt, remembering all he'd done for her, and forced his mouth to meet hers.

He stilled, then kissed her back gently, running his tongue over her swollen bottom lip. She nipped at his, laughing at her own recklessness.

Maybe on one count, Harris was right—risk *was* the price of progress. Could she allow those crumbling walls to stay down? Could she, perhaps, eradicate them completely?

Definitely, the drugs talking. She'd evaluate that another time.

For now, she relaxed into the warm male body lying

next to her. Tommy brushed a strand of hair from her face. "I love you, Tessa."

Love. Her heart danced around, the old panic trying to find something inside her to cling to. It failed, a warm sensation blooming there instead. Blinking, she smiled, allowing it to fill her up. "Good thing I love you, too, then."

He kissed her, this time slowly and deliberately.

When they broke apart, she poked him in the side. "That doesn't mean I'm not going after the swan position."

His deep chuckle made her smile. He tipped his forehead against hers. "You deserve it."

As she laid her head on his chest, he tucked her against him. A realization hit her, clear and undeniable.

She wasn't alone. She had Spence. Meg and Declan. Even Jessie.

She had a reason to live. A purpose. An odd but loyal family like she'd never had before.

And, for the first time ever, she realized as the warmth of Tommy's nearness began to lull her back to sleep, she had the right guy in her bed.

VISIT MY STORE

Did you know you can buy directly from me? When you do, the retailer doesn't take a cut and I can pass on the savings to YOU!

https://mistyevansbooks.com/shop

Benefits:

You can find ALL my books in one place

SAVE money

EARLY access to new releases

Special Collections, Boxed Sets, and Limited Editions

Support a small business (and support a dream!)

Why Buy Direct?

When you purchase a book by your favorite author, electronic or print, on retailer platforms, the company keeps 30-70% of the sale, leaving the author with little to no profit (after the company deducts delivery fees, taxes, and other fees).

Buying directly from the author means that more goes to them so they can keep turning out stories for you. Every published story, every book, requires cover art, editing, and hours and hours of the author's time simply to create it. Not to mention overhead costs, such as websites, newsletters, writing software, graphics programs, advertising, taxes, etc.

In addition, one of the big-name retailers requires exclusivity, and all of them have terms of service and rules and regulations that make it challenging and time-consuming for an indie author to navigate the publishing world.

Most of us would MUCH rather spend our time creating more stories for YOU, rather than trying to jump through the hoops at the retailers. Buying direct from your favorite authors (where available) helps ensure that an author you love is not subject to unexplained account closures, withholding of royalties, censorship, and other issues that can affect their livelihood.

I've experienced ALL of these. By buying direct, you help put control of my work back in my hands - and I can continue to write more.

Either way, thank you for supporting me! I understand buying direct doesn't work for everyone and even if you use the retailers to buy my books, I appreciate you!

Happy reading,

Misty

https://mistyevansbooks.com/shop

Don't want to miss a single release? Click here to join my reader list!

Black Swan Division Romantic Thriller Series

Redeeming Meg

Tempting Tessa

Avenging Jessie (Coming fall 2025)

SEALs of Shadow Force Series

Fatal Truth

Fatal Honor

Fatal Courage

Fatal Love

Fatal Vision

Fatal Thrill

Risk

SEALS of Shadow Force Series: Spy Division

Man Hunt

Man Killer

Man Down

Covert Affairs

Covert Tactics

Covert Obsession

The SCVC Taskforce Series

Deadly Pursuit

Deadly Deception

Deadly Force

Deadly Intent

Deadly Affair, A SCVC Taskforce novella

Deadly Attraction

Deadly Secrets

Deadly Holiday, A SCVC Taskforce novella

Deadly Target

Deadly Rescue

Deadly Bounty

Deadly Betrayal

Deadly Threat

The Super Agent Series

Operation Sheba

Operation Paris

Operation Proof of Life

Operation Lost Princess

Operation Ambush

Operation Contraband

Operation Sleeping With the Enemy

Operation Heist

The Justice Team Series (with Adrienne Giordano)

Stealing Justice

Cheating Justice

Holiday Justice

Exposing Justice

Undercover Justice

Protecting Justice

Missing Justice

Defending Justice

SCHOCK SISTERS MYSTERY SERIES w/Adrienne Giordano

1st Shock

2nd Strike

3rd Tango

4th Silence (Coming soon)

The Secret Ingredient Culinary Mystery Series

The Secret Ingredient, A Culinary Romantic Mystery with Bonus Recipes

The Secret Life of Cranberry Sauce, A Secret Ingredient Holiday Novella

Witches Anonymous Step 1

Jingle Hells, WA Step 2

Wicked Souls, WA Step 3

Dark Moon Lilith, Witches Anonymous Step 4

Dancing With the Devil, Witches Anonymous Step 5

Devil's Due, Witches Anonymous Step 6

Dirty Deeds, Witches Anonymous Step 7

Wicked Wedding, Witches Anonymous Step 8

Soul Survivor, Moon Water Series, Book 1

Soul Protector, Moon Water Series, Book 2

COZY MYSTERIES (WRITING AS NYX HALLIWELL)

Sister Witches Of Raven Falls Mystery Series

Of Potions and Portents

Of Curses and Charms

Of Stars and Spells

Of Spirits and Superstition

Confessions of a Closet Medium Series

Sister Witches of Story Cove Series

Cinder

Belle

Snow

Ruby

Zelle

Sister Witches of Story Cove Complete Set

***

Witchy Candy Shop Mysteries

Tricks and Treats

Candy and Creeps

Gum and Ghouls (releasing 2025)

MEET MISTY

USA TODAY Bestselling Author Misty Evans has published over ninety novels, as well as nonfiction inspirational journals. She loves writing urban fantasy, paranormal romance, and mystery/suspense. Under her pen name, Nyx Halliwell, she also writes supernatural cozy mysteries.

When not reading or writing, she enjoys music, movies, and hanging out with her husband, twin sons, and three spoiled rescue dogs. She's a crafter at heart and has far too many projects to finish.

Visit www.mistyevansbooks.com to check out her online store and sign up for her newsletter.

LETTER FROM MISTY

Thank you for reading this story! It is an honor and a privilege to write books for you. I'm an indie author and every fan is important to me. I pour my heart into each story and do my best to bring you an escape from the real world.

Readers are the key to my success - not a traditional publishing deal (had four), an agent (had two), or a publicity team (yep, you guessed it, had several of those as well.)

Those of you who read my books, love my characters and worlds, and then tell others about them are the best of friends. I adore you and will keep writing if you keep reading!

If you'd like to learn about my other books, sales, and special promotions, please sign up for my newsletter at **www.mistyevansbooks.com**.

You'll get coupons to download starter packs for FREE, whether you love my suspense or my paranormal.

Support me directly (no retailer taking their cut), grab special edition box sets, and get new releases before they are out at retailers by visiting my store **https://mistye vansbooks.com/shop**.

I have sales and offer NEW RELEASES early! Check it out.

Last but not least, if you enjoy clean, cozy mysteries, visit my pen name **www.nyxhalliwell.com** to see those books.

Thank you, and happy reading!

Misty

www.ingramcontent.com/pod-product-compliance
Lightning Source LLC
Chambersburg PA
CBHW020318260626
47156CB00004B/1282